TOP SHELF

Boston Rebels, book 1

_____

RJ SCOTT

V.L. LOCEY

Love Lane Books

Copyright

Top Shelf (Boston Rebels #1)

Copyright © 2021 RJ Scott, Copyright © 2021 V.L. Locey

Cover design by Meredith Russell, Edited by Kathy Krick

Published by Love Lane Books Limited

ISBN - 9781785645860

All Rights Reserved

Dedication

To my family who accepts me and all my foibles and quirks. Even the plastic banana in my holster.
VL Locey

Always for my family.
RJ Scott

TOP SHELF

BOSTON REBELS BOOK 1

RJ SCOTT & V.L. LOCEY

Love Lane Books

Chapter One

Xander

"I'M NOT ONE TO MAKE LONG FLOWERY SPEECHES. I LEAVE that to Dunny who loves to run off at the mouth. What I will say is that I've reached a point in my life where I can no longer hide who I am from the world or the fans nor do I wish to. I'm a bisexual man in a sport that is slowly— painfully slowly, it feels—growing in acceptance of LGBTQ players, thanks in no small part to the bravery of Tennant Rowe. Thank you for your time."

LESS THAN ONE HUNDRED WORDS SPOKEN BUT THOSE FEW sentences would forever change my life. For the good or for the bad remained to be seen. Judging by the looks of shock my best friend Eli Kingsley was wearing, I had to assume some of that bad was headed my way. And rightfully so.

I'd kept my private life locked down *tight*.

No one had known I was bisexual because on the odd occasion I dated, it was women, and really it's not anyone's business what I get up to behind bedroom doors. So, yeah, no one knew anything. Not the team or my parents. No. One.

Of course, there had been a few men, meaningless hookups, whom I'd used to scratch the itch, but they'd not known who I was. Dark bathrooms, no names exchanged, bust a nut and leave without a thank you slaking of basic needs thing. I'd thought I'd been careful. Fuck, I *had* been careful. Giving some rando a blowjob in an alley at night while wearing sunglasses and a ballcap was sadly cliché and always left a bad taste in my mouth. Pun sort of intended.

Seems I wasn't as clever as I'd thought. Rando guy from a month ago in Columbus had taken note of the tattoo on my wrist when he'd been on his knees in a slimy men's room in a tacky gay bar. It wasn't a large tat or anything bright or flashy. Xander Holden didn't do flashy. It was just a small fish. A memento of a summer getaway with my folks. I'd taken them to Hawaii and after a few cocktails—okay—my mother and I had gotten inked. Dad had gone to sleep off his mai tais and had missed the drunken tattoo talk. Mom had gotten a pretty little tropical fish on her left wrist. I'd gotten a tribal design koi chasing its tail. Nothing gaudy. Xander Holden, aka the man in the closet, didn't do gaudy either.

How the fuck this rando guy had known who I was simply by spying my koi tattoo while I was stroking his jaw as he sucked me off, I have no clue. It had been so murky and shadowed in the stall, I could barely see my dick between his lips. But he'd somehow figured it out. He did the two plus two and within two days of that shitty BJ, he'd contacted me on Twitter via personal messenger and asked for money to keep my secret.

One short DM and my life had crumbled around me. I refused to call the cops and I refused to be bullied. I played hockey for the Boston Rebels. Defensemen for the original six teams did not allow themselves to be bullied. So I took a day to cry alone in my condo, then I beat the asshole to the punch. They can't blackmail you if the whole world knows the secret. I'd taken a personal day and flown down to Tampa where my parents lived and told them everything. They'd been incredibly accepting but hurt that I'd not felt able to tell them when I was a teen. And now I was seeing that same pain in Eli's eyes. And it sucked.

Brady, the Rebels captain and my defensive partner, and Nick, team owner, hustled me away from the press. I wasn't taking questions. I'd told them I was bi and that was all they were getting out of me on the subject.

"Team meeting," Brady announced as my teammates silently trudged along behind me. "Mr. Sinclair wants all of us in the video room in ten minutes. No calls to family are allowed until after this meeting."

Good old Brady. The poor bastard. I'd laid this on him yesterday after morning skate. Then I'd ridden up to Nick Sinclair's posh office overlooking the ice with my captain/diversity union rep at my side to drop the bomb on Sinclair. To say that the always volatile Nicolaus Icarus Sinclair took the news well would have been a lie. Nick tended to explode with little provocation. I assumed it was his Mediterranean blood that gave him such fire. The man was still smoldering today, but the inferno had died down.

"I need to talk to you a minute," Eli said as we made our way to the video room. I nodded. It was only right I give him some personal time. He'd been my best friend since we'd been toddlers. We'd grown up together, lived side-by-side, had both skipped college to come to Boston to play. We were as tight as he was with his younger brother, Mason. He of the sensual eyes and lush lips. Mason. The one man who I shouldn't be so damn attracted to and yet... yeah, and yet. Even thinking about the way his eyes sparkled when he smiled or the way he tipped his head when in thought was off-limits. He was Eli's baby brother. One didn't wheel a fellow teammate's little sister or brother. And one most certainly did not wheel a best friend's sibling. That was asking for drama I didn't need at the moment.

Shaking off the image of Eli's brother, I led him into the skate sharpening room. No one was here, obviously. Everyone had been at my presser. Everyone except my agent who'd dropped me when I'd called him yesterday to tell him I was bi. Or rather I dropped him when all he could say was that I'd better stay quiet and just date women because bi wasn't a real thing. Guess ten years of him getting ten percent of everything I earned wasn't enough to buy me some respect or understanding. I suspected I would lose more than an agent before this all settled down.

Eli closed the door then leaned on it, his eyes glittering with pain. I studied the racks of skates needing attention.

When I finally looked back at him, his lips were as thin as a papercut.

"I'm sorry for not telling you," I blurted out.

"Yeah, well, I appreciate that, but it still hurts that you hid this from me for… forever!" Eli snapped then drew in a long breath and closed his eyes. "Sorry. I didn't mean to get loud. I know how hard it is for people to come out. Mason kept it from everyone for a few years until he was ready, so I get it but still, Xan, man it hurts. I won't lie. Fucking Brady knew before I did."

I drew in a slow breath. "I had to tell him. He's the diversity rep *and* our captain *and* my defensive partner." His eyes rounded. "I know you're my best friend, but I had to get a handle on something in a hurry."

"What thing? The bi thing?" He folded his arms across his chest, his forearms resting on the revolutionary war eagle that was our Rebels logo. "I knew something was off with you. You've been so damn angry at the world forever."

I had been? Okay, yeah, that was a fair call.

"No, well yeah, but… some guy I hooked up with wanted five hundred grand, or he would tell the press that I was into guys."

His jaw dropped. "Holy fucking hell, Xan."

I shrugged. Then I filled him in as quickly as possible. Sinclair wanted to talk to us and the smell of all these sweaty skates was becoming overpowering.

"I hate people," Eli grumbled after the sordid tale was told.

"Yeah, I'm not too fond of people at the moment either. Maybe I'll just become a monk." Eli snorted and it was that stupid sound that told me we'd be okay. Eventually. "If it helps, my parents just found out three days ago."

"Jesus. For a guy who shuns attention… "

"Yeah, I know. Trust me, this was not how I wanted my coming out to go."

"I get that, buddy." He uncrossed his arms so he could grab my shoulders. Our eyes met and held. "And if I ever find out who this asshole is I'll drop a hammer on him. I might not be a big, bad D-man like you, but I can kick ass when warranted. And if anyone on the ice gets lippy about you being queer my fist will find their face. Just putting that out there."

"Thanks. That means a lot." I got a little emotional. Eli gave my shoulders a squeeze. "It's great that you're willing to toss the gloves for me but maybe you should let me handle any instigators. Remember the last time you threw down with Adler Lockhart? The dude whipped you like a rug."

Eli made that pig-like snort sound. "In my defense, he caught me unaware with some stupid joke about a rabbit, a priest, and minister walking into a bar. While I was trying to figure out whether he meant rabbit or rabbi, he sucker punched me in the face."

"Dude, that was no sucker punch. People in the rafters saw it coming."

Eli tugged me into his chest. We bro hugged for a long time then we broke apart. "We better get to that meeting, but we're not done discussing this. And don't ever hide shit from me again. We made a blood pact."

I smiled. The first smile to grace my face in days. "I won't do it again."

"Okay then. Let's go see what Sinclair has to say to us."

We gave each other one more hug then hurried to the video room. Coach Franks met me at the door, chunky scarred hand extended. I shook the old defenseman's hand. All eyes rested on us. Austin and Brady Rowe stood and began clapping. Soon the entire room was on its feet aside from Nick Sinclair, who had draped his slim frame over a rolling desk chair. I ducked my head. Eli clapped me on the back then we dropped into our usual seats. I hated attention. I wasn't here to dance in the spotlight. I was here to play hockey. That was it.

Nick got to his feet, tugged down his expensive suit jacket, and ran a hand over his ebony hair. He was a handsome son-of-a-bitch. Lean, not overly tall but not super short, always full of spunk and energy which would do him well as he'd taken over all his late father's vast holdings, including a hockey team. Not too bad for a man not even forty years old yet. He wasn't my type at all, but his smoldering dark looks and designer clothes won him the eye of many. Being one of the richest men in Massachusetts didn't hurt his appeal either.

"You know I'm not one to beat around the bush so I'm going to say it right out. I've been known to knock boots with guys on occasion myself. If anyone in this room wants to make it known to the team and or the Rebels management that they're LGBTQ, now is a great time to free yourselves. This is an inclusive organization. We do not tolerate hate in our hallowed halls. The first time I hear of anyone using a racial or phobic slur of any kind your ass is grass, and I will be the motherfucking lawnmower. I have zero tolerance for hateful shit in any business I run." Sinclair looked out at the room. "I'm not forcing anyone to come out. I wouldn't do that, and I can't legally. What I'm asking is that if you decide to make any announcements, let me know beforehand please and try to give me more than twenty-four hours' notice. I'm not a fan of last-minute surprises. Dry humps suck." He looked at me. I nodded in understanding.

Trust me, boss, if I would've had a choice I'd have handled it with far more reserve and grace. Or maybe stayed in the closet until I'd retired.

"Just wanted to get that out there. Feel free to talk to Brady if you have something bothering you or come to me or the team counselor. We'll have your backs," Nick said and then looked at each of us with those dark, dark eyes of his until his gaze settled on Austin. The poor kid withered under the owner's attention then he raised a hand.

"I have a boyfriend," Austin said softly. There was really no surprise there.

Dunny stood up. "I like dick." The room exploded in laughter. Dunny chuckled. "Well, I do. I like pussy too. Hell, I'll boink anything that's got a pulse."

"Someone lock up the sheep!" someone shouted from the back of the room.

Nick glowered. Coach Franks pinched the bridge of his nose. Brady was struggling to maintain his captainly composure. As the laughter settled, our soft-spoken goalie got to his feet. Renco rubbed the back of his neck, his gaze flickering around the room just as it did when he was doing his ocular warm-ups before a game. We all waited for him to speak but he simply made some vague motion with his hand that looked like ASL to me. He tended to do that a lot as his older sister was deaf, so I think it was second nature to him at times.

"Queer," he said as an afterthought then sat down.

Our newest acquisition from Detroit to play rightwing on the third line, Marquis Miller, got to his shiny brown boots and tugged at the collar of his African print turtleneck sweater. Marquis had been voted one of the best-dressed players in the NHL three years in a row by magazines that do that kind of fashion thing. I never saw him in anything that wasn't trendy or well put together. And he never wore a beanie, but he'd wear those old 40s style hats. Trendsetter they said.

People in the press talk about Nick, his family, their connections, and how they got their money. Lots of talk of Greek mafia ties that his grandfather had established before leaving Greece. I had no clue if the Stavropolous— which became Sinclair when his family arrived in America for reasons unknown—had ties to unsavory sorts or not, but Nick knew hockey. And he was making trades that would aid us in our quest for another Cup. Including the fashionable Marquis, who looked like a beefy Jon Batiste and played one hell of a physical game.

"I'm pan," Marquis announced then sat back down as smooth as silk.

"You guys are killing me here." Nick sounded so forlorn.

I understood where he was coming from. My announcement today was going to stir up some real shit that our PR team would be trying to shine up for palatability for weeks, if not months. The common fan wouldn't be impressed as the *common fan* was male and white and more than likely straight. Professional sports were the last bastion of masculinity according to some, and the raging hetero boys clung to their outdated homophobic biases with vigor. Sure, we'd made some strides. Tennant Rowe had forced others to look at queer players with new respect as had many of his teammates and a few players out in Arizona. So while I wasn't the lone target for the haters, I was going to be the newest one. And that could translate to empty seats.

"Coach, they're all yours now. Oh, and we ask you all not to comment publicly on Xander's announcement unless it's to say you're an ally and fully support your teammate. If you don't feel that way, fine, that's your right but do not spout hateful rhetoric to the press or fans. And for the love of my grandmother's fasolatha keep your views to yourself on social media."

Nick left, and our attention turned to Coach Franks as he walked over to the light switch. "So, I think we all know where the team stands on today's announcement. Keep in mind that we're a team. We play as one and we support each other. With that said, since we're all here let's spend the next hour doing our jobs."

The lights went off, the video screen lit up, and we put aside the shitstorm brewing outside to do that hockey thing we got paid to do.

Chapter Two

Mason

"HOLD THIS," BECCA CLARKE PASSED ME HER TRAY OF snacks then wriggled around, making herself comfortable. I took the chance to dig out a couple of chips that weren't covered in every topping imaginable and snaffled them before she noticed. She might be my best friend, but she was rigorously territorial about snacks. She straightened her Rebels jersey, smoothing the C on the front and then sending a kiss to the heavens, one of those good luck things that she swore helped toward a Rebels win. She had Brady Rowe's number on her back. Her jersey was from his first year as captain and she treasured it almost as much as she loved her snacks.

I had Eli's number on my back because I was the best little brother in the entire world, and his biggest fan, although I'd never tell him that. I'd looked up to Eli since I knew what a big brother was, and despite the lean years when I was an annoying brat and he was too cool for me, we were very close. Him playing for the Rebels would've sent our parents into a frenzy given they'd been true-blue New York fans, but they'd never gotten to see him play.

I was fifteen when our parents died and nineteen year old Eli had become my guardian, a pseudo parent who didn't know how to back off. He fussed and corralled and took me all over the country with him until I was old enough to go to college and then get a job.

Not that I'd moved far from him given I lived in Eli's pool house free of charge and had no college loans to pay off. Being the little brother of a millionaire pro skater had its pluses. I would pay him back every cent one day, but it wasn't happening now. In contrast to Becca's fading jersey, I wore the newest design I could get my hands on because hey, I got perks, and Eli had a ton of them just sitting in his office. The only shitty thing was that it also had some minuses.

Like the fact I was hopelessly in love with my brother's best friend—Boston's world-class pushy irritatingly perfect D-Man, Xander *freaking* Holden.

Eli and Xander had been more like brothers than friends, close since they were old enough to hold a stick. Luck had made them teammates, but love and respect kept them in each other's lives.

Lives that included me in a ton of different ways. I used to follow them everywhere, the boy who played hockey but didn't really love it, the annoying and whiny one. My brother loved me the most, our connection was family, but for a long time, he'd rather have spent time with Xander than me.

I never told him that I'd also rather spend time with

Xander because what had begun as hero worship had taken a turn to adoration of a very different kind. Knowing I was gay was one thing, coming to terms with how Eli and I fit together in the brotherly dynamic after my announcement another, but when love for Xander hit me, it hit hard, and every part of teenage Mason fell for him in the worst way.

It was a futile love, the kind that was featured in older gay romances where there was never a happy ending. He would never be my boyfriend. He hugged me as a friend, teased me, ganged up on me with Eli, but he was straight, and had girlfriends, and was never going to be *mine*.

Only, everything had changed. Three weeks ago, without any warning, Xander revealed he wasn't straight at all. In a goddamn public to the world news conference, he'd told the world he was bisexual. That he *liked men*. I was blindsided, hurt, but when I saw my brother's expression as he listened to the news, I could see Eli hadn't known a thing about it. It wasn't just me then that had his whole world turned upside down.

The day I told Eli that I was gay he simply shrugged, said it was cool, but I always recall what he said when we hugged. *It's not as if you want to play hockey as a career, so you can just be yourself.*

Becca settled in next to me and took back the nachos, eyeing me suspiciously as if she was checking for crumbs. I feigned innocence and after a moment, she was lured away from staring by the call of synthetic cheese and chilies. Then it must have occurred to her that the teams would be out for warm-ups soon and I was still in my seat.

"Adhhdnsmpph?" she asked around a mouth of crunch.

"Not doing it tonight," I answered because after years

of sitting next to her at the arena, I could speak fluent nacho-ese. She hurried to finish the mouthful and nearly choked at the speed.

"What?" She wiped her mouth with the paper towel. "No. You *have* to go down there and do the thing," she said, and there was very real fear in her voice. As if me going down to the glass was really Eli and Xander's good luck *thing* before a home game. "It's the finals!" she added with as much shock in her voice as if I'd told her I'd killed a puppy.

"Maybe I'm actually bad luck?" I suggested, and her eyes widened. "What if I don't want to do the *thing*?" I settled back into my chair, and she stared at me.

"But you *have to.* Without you doing the thing the Rebels will lose game one."

"That's blatantly untrue." I gave her my best *whatever* look, and she thumped me on the arm. She pouted then pulled her lip between her teeth and gave me her puppy dog expression, the one I normally did everything to avoid. When I didn't say anything, she even added a small please.

"Becca—"

"There's plexiglass between you and Xander," she explained as if I hadn't thought about that.

"The last thing I want to do is… " I waved a hand to the glass that was four rows below us, gesturing to the empty ice. This was the first game I'd attended since Xander's presser, always finding just the right excuse to avoid being at the games, to the point that Becca had to drag me out of the house tonight, insisting I had to go since it was the first in the Stanley Cup Finals. This final push was best of seven against a strong LA team, but the first game of a series was always important and Boston had home advantage.

"You told me you're over him," Becca said right next to my ear, and I winced at the memory. I had said exactly that, and for a few seconds, I'd actually meant it. Xander featured heavily in my late night fantasies and in every one of them he had abruptly realized he was into me, and we would fuck like rabbits, fall in love, have kids, and a dog. In those dreams, he loved me back as much as I loved him. They were imaginative nothings just to get myself off, or at least that is what I told myself.

"I was lying," I muttered, and she elbowed me.

"Well, I know that." The implied *duh* was in the roll of her eyes. "But unless you tell him of your big unrequited love then how will he know?"

I shook my head because he'd had all this time to tell me he was into men as well as women, let me down gently, or explain to me how we could have an affair behind closed doors. There was a ton of things he *could* have done.

I checked around myself and lowered my voice again. "Maybe I only think I'm in love because I was safe in the knowledge that he would never return the feelings?"

"Jeez, Mase!" She was pissed with me, but that was probably more to do my refusal to do the warm-up ritual which in her eyes gave the Rebels supposed luck. "Go down there, smile at him, and put yourself out there."

How in God's name was I going to face Xander? All this time I'd been flirting with him in my own way, and I thought it was going right over his head, but if he was attracted to men and he'd seen the flirting and thought…

oh holy hell... I could feel my face heating. Xander was the reason I couldn't get a sentence out in the correct order whenever I was near him in fear that he would realize I was crushing on him and laugh, and now he's telling the world that all this time he was playing for my team.

Fuck my life.

I was angry at him, and supportive of him, and angry again, then embarrassed, and then I wanted to hug him, then punch him, then hug him again. Twenty-one days since the presser and I'd run nearly the entire gamut of every emotion with my love for all things Xander Holden. The only thing I hadn't felt was hope that he would see me as anything other than his best friend's little brother because he'd been bi all this time, and if he hadn't yet swept me off my Nikes, then it wasn't going to happen now just because he was out.

There was only one other person in this entire world who knew how I felt, and that was Becca. She had this crazy sixth sense for things I was hiding, and five years back she'd caught me staring at his picture in the program at a game. We'd been handed passes to meet the guys after a game, perks of being in the family, had good seats to watch all the action, and there I was staring at his picture. She said I looked like a cat staring at cream... she wasn't wrong.

A few beers later at a raucous bar, watching Xander and Eli leave with women on their arms, I'd lost my head and admitted to my best friend exactly how I felt. It was cathartic, but it also led to a whole new thread in our friendship, one where she had a new determination to get me to tell Xander how I felt.

Like that *was going to happen.*

All I'd done since hearing him say his truth was fret and get angry, and even avoided social gatherings where I'd have to talk to him, and what was that about? The one time I'd actually plucked up the courage to start a conversation about him coming out, my brother had ambled over and gave me a noogie before pushing me in the pool. Things had become awkward, and there was also the way that Xander was avoiding me right back. The last thing he would want is me down by the glass doing our *thing* when he didn't even want to look at me when he was in the house, let alone talk to me.

What's the worst that can happen if I do go down there?

That was easy. Xander Holden, the man who held my heart in his hands, could skate rapidly in the opposite direction, and I'd be left staring at his very fine hockey butt.

"You need to talk to him." She leaned in as she gave me her latest piece of wisdom and kept her voice low. We didn't know the people sitting closest to us, but the arena was still filling so the seats around us were mostly empty. We just had to be careful because with some of the shit I'd read in forums revolving around Xander coming out, I didn't want to add myself as a problem to the anti-gay sentiment swelling from some parts of the media and the crowd. We'd made it to the finals by the skin of our teeth, with a rag-tag group of exhausted and injured men, and no one really expects us to beat a hot LA team.

"No I don't."

"Well, you need to before the big vay-cay," she air

quoted the last part in an effort to highlight the one flaw in my plan to avoid Xander. Eli had corralled me into helping him organize a surprise birthday party for Xander's thirtieth, which was coming up soon. I'd found the hotel, scouted for things to do, tried everything to make it special for the three of us, and had a long list of excuses ready for me to get out of doing things with them.

I groaned. "Don't remind me."

I was in love with him when I thought he was straight and unattainable. Now he was bi and single, and my lizard brain just wanted him under me, in me, over me, then next to me for the rest of my life.

I have it so bad.

"You have to tell him before you go, at least. I mean, you can't get to the island and then hide in your room the entire freaking time and ignore him just in case he notices how you feel."

Becca was right. Birthdays were momentous, and this was a big one. I hadn't seen Xander hook up with a guy yet, so I had a chance. Right?

I'd considered talking to Eli, and even though Eli was an asshole at times, he would do *anything* for me. I was his priority, and if he found out I'd approached Xander about how I felt, he would feel betrayed, weirded out, but I know he would eventually forgive me for breaking the unspoken rule.

He would *never* forgive Xander. Not after everything that happened at the same party where the popcorn incident had taken place. I turned eighteen, got into a fight with Becca, and had to fend off an unwanted and physical advance from a hockey player that left me shaken. I'd persuaded Eli it was nothing, but how Eli hadn't killed the guy I don't know. I wouldn't forget Aarni Lankinen in a hurry, and worse, neither would Eli. Super protective big brother turned into his own branch of the boyfriend police.

And if he knew I'd fallen for Xander to the point where my heart wasn't my own, what would he do? Xander played hockey, but he was a good guy. Xander was a defenseman who was like a brick wall, had more than one fight, hip-checked like a beast, and protected his team with his body, but *he was a good guy.*

It was too late to talk anymore, the team was coming out for warm-ups, and Becca gripped my arm. "Please, Mase?"

I rolled my eyes just to let her know this was against my better judgment and then jumped the four steps to glass level and bypassed some of the fans there with posters asking for pucks from various players. Mostly from the new kid, Austin Rowe, who was a pretty blond guy with a boyfriend, and also a hell of a player. I reached my spot just as the black and gold spilled onto the ice, and as soon as they saw I was there, Eli and Xander headed my way. There was this complicated fist bump thing the three of us did, the same as I'd done with them when I was six, and the routine of it ended with them high fiving each other, leaning in and doing that chainsaw quote thing they did.

When Eli skated off to shoot a few pucks, Xander stayed right at the glass and tilted his head in question as if he was examining me. Unbidden I pressed my hand flat to the plexiglass, and he nodded. God knows what any of that meant, but the butterflies in my stomach were flapping and smashing into each other, and I turned away from the ice and headed back to Becca on wobbly legs. I semi-collapsed into my seat, sliding down until I could hide my face in my hands. What had I just done, putting my hand on the glass like that? As if Xander and I had a connection that actually meant something past being family friends.

"Mason! Becca!"

We both turned to face the woman who called our names, and a smile replaced the angst. The Blakes were here. Mom, momma, and toddler twins, one of the first surrogacy cases that I'd been handed to work through myself with Becca on the team. The first, but not the last, same-sex case we'd been handed. The downfall of working for the conservative and uber traditional Franklin Agency was that the words same and sex used together were abhorrent to the owners. What the agency did love though was that these new clients brought with them a whole new income stream that couldn't be ignored. The hypocrisy was barefaced, and obvious to our clients, and was why Becca and I were branching out with our own agency. We wanted a place dedicated to all kinds of cases, not just same-sex parents, but single parents, and in fact, anything else that didn't fit into the remit of the Franklin Agency and their strict and stuffy rules.

The Blake twins looked so cute in tiny Rebels jerseys, and the moms showed us a homemade sign proclaiming this was the twins' first game. I'd make sure to get them a couple of pucks, and after I waved at the kids, I sent a quick text to Eli that I knew he would pick up after the game.

"Did you write your resignation letter?" I blurted because I sure as hell needed to change the conversation away from hockey, and Xander, and being hopelessly in love with the unattainable.

"Yep. You?"

"It's done."

She reached out and took my hand, squeezing it in reassurance. We were both turning in our notices at the end of next month, and that was big. Huge.

That was what I needed to focus on. Not the game, not the upcoming vacation which was going to be frustratingly awkward. And certainly not Xander.

Chapter Three

Xander

FOUR MINUTES AND EIGHT SECONDS.

We'd lost games one, two and three, and now this was the amount of time we had to turn this train wreck of a series around. How we'd gotten ourselves into this situation was still up for speculation. Many sports writers cited fatigue and injuries, and that was no lie. Every Boston Rebel was exhausted and hurt. Some bloggers called out the coaching staff for egregious errors with shuffling lines. Many thought we were suffering from the curse that befell any team that touched the Prince of Wales trophy. Which might have some merit. I cop to being a superstitious hockey player. Although Brady had touched it the previous two years we'd won the Cup so yeah, maybe not. Who knows.

A few members of the press had called into question my ability to play a man's game like hockey since I was, in their words, not straight. My coming out was still causing some ripples. Nothing huge now, that had taken place right after the surprise announcement, but I was still a curiosity to some it seemed. If only I had been able to be my true self at nineteen as Austin Rowe had. No hoopla, just moving gently into public life with his boyfriend. There had been barely an eyebrow raised which was fantastic. We had come a long way for sure, but there was still work to be done. Hopefully coming out would go the way of the rotary phone and VHS tapes soon and we could all just live and love as we damn pleased.

But until those days arrived, we had to deal with bigoted people and ignorant reporters making sly—and not so sly at times—digs about a gay man's masculinity. Those I ignored, or tried to, but they stung like a blocked slapshot to the groin. No matter what the reason turned out to be for our fall from grace, we were now looking at four minutes to get our asses in gear and save the series. We did not want to go home to Boston after suffering a sweep in the Stanley Cup Finals. We could not go home after a sweep. We *would* not go home after a sweep.

I took another swig of water to cleanse the taste of lactic acid from my mouth. I looked at the massive crowd packed into the Grantsman Arena here in downtown Los Angeles and dug deep into the well to try to find something to say to the team during this brief TV timeout. Anything to invigorate them. There was no time to start a fight, and to do so at this juncture, with the score sitting at 1-0, would have been suicidal. I carried enough shit for being out. I didn't need the shame of a penalty for a stupid mistake to add to the veiled and sometimes not-so-veiled digs.

"Okay, guys, we got this!" I shouted to be heard over the roaring hometown fans. Brady, our captain and my defensive partner, was in a world of hurt and too gassed to speak. Yet, here he was, shoulder iced, playing hockey. Usually, it would be him talking us up, but he had all he could do not to puke judging by the pallor of his skin and the papercut set to his lips. As one of the two alternate captains, I stepped up. "Four minutes. You know how many goals we can score in four minutes? A shitload, that's how many. We just need one break, a bit of puck luck, to turn this around. We win here tonight, and we go back home. Then we take it to this bunch of pretty boy movie stars!"

The men rallied around the pep talk with as much enthusiasm as they could muster. Coach barked at us to stay tight in the corners and focus on winning faceoffs. My line nodded, put in our mouthguards, and skated back out to take the faceoff. Brady and I hung back, letting Eli and the wingers roll in tight.

Eli and I exchanged a look, both of us whispering "I'll bring the chainsaw" to the other. It was an old ritual of ours that started back when we were kids and obsessed with the old *Tango & Cash* movie with Sly Stallone and Kurt Russell. That line, we felt at the age of eight, was every fucking thing and summarized how kickass we really were.

I stood next to a big bruiser of a D-man from LA who'd ridden me and Brady hard all night long. Eli won the faceoff, shuttling the puck back to Brady, who then hustled his ass down the ice. I was in hot pursuit, my legs burning with fatigue, when the man I was supposed to be covering broke free and knocked Brady off the puck. And I mean he checked our captain so hard Rowe yelped in pain. His shout lost amid the cheers of the fans, as the man I'd dropped fired the puck behind the net. Our goalie, Renco, moved left to plant his skate to the pipe, but the puck had already been passed to the LA captain who split the defenders, then fired a wrist short to send the puck into the top shelf of the net. The red light flared to life. And my team collapsed in on itself.

I fished the puck out of the net and skated back to the bench, the weight of a defeat now weighing heavily on every Rebel. Our captain left the bench with the trainer then, and that sucked out whatever spark might have remained in us. The rest of the game was an exercise in futility. We continued to scrabble around like midget players instead of professionals. The LA goalie stood on his head, as he'd done throughout the first three games, and when the final countdown came and the confetti fell from the rafters, we all lowered our heads in shame.

Eli and I looked at each other after the misery of the loss eased a bit. I could see the pain of our defeat in his eyes, and I was sure he saw the same in mine.

How would we ever face the fans back home in Boston? Shit, how would we face ourselves? Those were questions for later though. Right now, we had a handshake line to endure. Moving along with Eli right behind me, as always, following Brady who was white as a sheet, we congratulated each LA player, clapped them on the shoulder, and told them how well they'd played. Then we moved off the ice to the away locker room to let the new champs bask in their well-earned glory.

"I wasn't expecting it to go top shelf," Renco repeated for the tenth time. "I thought he was going five hole."

"We let you down," Brady murmured, "let them get too close."

"Damn *fucking* top *fucking* shelf," Renco snapped, and then subsided back into his wide cubby.

Coach Franks made a nice speech. I made a speech. Brady came limping in with his arm in a sling, and he made a speech. But all the speeches in the world couldn't cure the blues we were all feeling. Only time could do that.

A WEEK LATER I STOOD IN THE BACK YARD OF ELI'S FANCY home out in Sharon, a suburb of Boston, drink in hand, wishing I'd just stayed home. Attending the end of the season shindig was mandatory, even after the hellacious week we'd just endured. It was a way of wrapping the season and celebrating the successes we had achieved. We'd made it to the finals. We'd gone further than all the other teams in the league save one. We should take those as wins. It wasn't our time to win the cup and there was always next year.

It still feels like the worst thing.

I sipped my rum and Coke and watched the younger players making fools of themselves in and around Eli's inground pool, seeing how easily they'd all bounced back after the loss. Was it just the ones like me, coming up on thirty, who wondered if we'd ever see another Cup run? There was change coming on this team, we were close to cap space and trades could happen over the summer.

Nobody was really safe, but that was hockey. For now, I needed to concentrate on being with the team, so I sat in the shade and people watched. Some of the family guys arrived, wives and kids in tow, but it wasn't them that caught my attention. Trailing behind them was the one man I was hoping wouldn't attend.

Mason Kingsley, younger brother of my best friend, Eli, and temptation dressed in shorts and a tank to show off his toned arms.

Back when Eli and I were mischievous rink rats in St. Cloud, Mason was the quintessential annoying younger brother. A pest, a nuisance, always underfoot. As a younger brother myself, I was well aware of all the tricks of the trade. We doled out a lot of abuse to Mason back then, as kids will, but he never gave up no matter how many times we ditched him. Next day there he would be, eager and wiggly like a beagle puppy anticipating playtime.

Mason had grown up into a young man with a charming personality, a smile that could melt the coldest heart, and a love of children and helping others. He'd finally filled out the gangly frame he'd stumbled around in during his teenage years and was now a lanky, well-made man with hazel eyes that twinkled when he talked to me and a dimple that made conversing with him more and more difficult the older he became. He waved at me and smiled. I waved back, but that was it. He ended up on the other side of the pool chatting with Becca, his coworker and best friend. It was for the best that he didn't come anywhere near me because ever since I'd held the press conference, it seemed I'd lost the ability to speak to him without tripping over my tongue. I'd spent so long pretending, that when the pretense fell, it left me exposed and needy, and it was Mason who kept filling my thoughts.

When I came out he sent me a simple text telling me he was there if I wanted to talk. I sent a thank you but since that day something between us had changed, and now we barely talked about anything at all. A hello if he saw me in passing, that ritual fist bump if he was watching a game, but I avoided him, and it wasn't as if he was demanding to see me.

Probably for the best.

Mason had been out for years. It had taken me longer as a professional athlete to work up the courage to step out of the closet, and no one had known. He was probably as pissed as Eli had been when I told him, but whereas Eli was pissed I hadn't confided in him, which quickly turned to complete support, Mason probably saw me as a coward for hiding as long as I had.

Now whenever I saw him, and that was all the damn time as I was always at Eli's place, this pulse of desire began to throb and beat between us. At first, it freaked me the hell out and still did to some extent. Eli would come unglued if I touched his baby brother. My bedding Mason could ruin a lifelong friendship and possibly seep into the locker room.

"You look as if you just licked the bottom of a dumpster." I pulled my gaze from Mason to find Brady standing beside me holding a can of soda and sporting a spiffy gold and black Rebels sling for his injured shoulder.

"Just thinking about shit. When are you going in for surgery?" I jerked my still hairy chin at his left arm. Most of the guys had removed the playoff beard, but I was clinging to mine for some reason. Not ready to move on yet, I guessed. Also, the dark beard looked good on me, I thought. And with no special someone to complain about it, I'd just trimmed it up this morning instead of shaving it off.

"Two weeks. This is my fourth surgery in what? Three years?"

I nodded. His shoulder issues were well known. Of course, he wasn't a spring chicken as my mother would say. He was closing in on thirty-four now. Hockey was hell on a body. I could attest to that. My knees ached on rainy days, and I was still a mass of bruises from blocking shots and knocking heads in the playoffs.

"You're a tough nut though. Heal up over the summer and when training camp opens you'll be out there skating rings around the young pups," I said with a smile. He made a sound into his soda can, taking a drink before replying. Someone tossed a lawn chair into the pool. Eli blew a gasket at them from the shadows where he'd been chatting up some girl.

"Maybe, I'm not so sure, Holdy." My gaze flicked from the lawn chair floating in the pool to Mason, his gaze boldly touching then holding mine. *Why is he looking at me that way?* "I might hang up my skates. The wife is worried, the kids are worried, my family is worried. I'm worn out, you know?"

Hearing the captain talk this way was shocking as was the fact that Mason was still staring at me. I wasn't sure which was more bewildering. Brady was supposed to be my captain for much longer. He was still so young. And

Mason had never spent so long looking right at me. *What the hell was going on with him?*

"Come on, you don't mean that." I chose to focus on Brady for now and after Mason returned his attention to Becca, I turned to look at my captain. "You're just in pain, Brady. Once you've had the surgery—"

"They're saying it might not heal as well this time. If not, it'll be a complete overhaul with a new shoulder replacement as I busted up the last one." His handsome face was tight with worry and a sad sort of resolution. "I'm just… " He glanced skyward. "I'm tired. My body is worn out. I miss my wife and kids. Then there's the rumors about the team trading me—"

"They're just rumors—"

"Can you imagine starting now at another team? In the kind of pain I'm in? I just… well, I guess I'm just at a crossroads."

"Shit," I murmured, tossing back a large gulp of my drink. I'd always thought Brady Rowe would be my partner forever. We just clicked. From the first time we'd played together seven years ago when I'd come to Boston fresh from college. God above, how the time had flown. I'd be thirty in a month and still living alone. No partner, no kids, not even a damn dog. "Shit, man, I just don't know what to say."

He nudged me with the sweaty can of lemon-lime soda in his hand. "Don't say anything to the other guys. I'm just talking. I know what I say to you is locked down tight."

"Totally. Always. You know that."

He gave me a wobbly smile. "And if I do decide to

retire, for what it's worth, I'll support you for the captaincy."

"I—"

He didn't let me speak. "No, don't act up about it. You've really matured into a great alternate, and your drive and dedication to the sport and this city will be a boon to the club. You'd make a great captain. Not as good as me of course, but… " He went to shrug then grimaced. "Shit that hurts."

"Ass," I teased, patting him on the biceps. "Thanks for the vote of confidence. I think there are better players on the team than me, but if I were to get the C, I would be deeply honored."

"Yeah, I knew you would be. So, I'm slipping out before any more furniture ends up in the pool and it all gets out of hand. Call me later." He made the hand gesture for calling, handed me his unfinished soda, and then snuck off into the night. Home to his beautiful wife and children and his old dog named Bourque. I drained the soda into the flower bed, finished my drink, and made to exit the same way Brady had, but I took a quick detour into the pool house to use the bathroom before I made the thirty-minute ride back to my condo on Beacon Street.

I'd been in the pool house a hundred times over the years so finding the bathroom in the dimly lit home was like finding my face. After using the toilet and washing up, I gave myself a long look in the mirror. I'd been feeling down for a while now. The brutal loss to LA in the finals had only ramped up my blues. But now I was feeling a little less beleaguered. I'd not been kidding when I'd said I'd be honored to wear the big C on my left shoulder. So many greats had worn that letter over the years. It would be a privilege to follow in their footsteps. Knowing Brady felt I had what it takes to lead the team bolstered my flagging self-esteem. Running my fingers through my brown hair, the same shade as my mother's, I studied my face, patted my cheeks with wet hands, and decided I wasn't all that ugly. Aside from the scar on my chin from a skate blade four years ago, hidden under my beard, I was passable. Nothing as striking as Mason with his dark hair and hazel eyes. Mine were a muddy shade of brown, again like my mother's. Those eyes of Mason's were enthralling. Pools of green and brown with flecks of gold that a man could wade out into and spend an eternity swimming in.

"Enough of that, Xander Mills Holden. This isn't *Pride and Prejudice*," I whispered in my best motherly tone, dried my hands, and opened the door. Mason stood outside, back against the wall, waiting to use the bathroom. The sizzle that seemed to engulf us whenever we were near sparked to life as soon as the aroma of his citrus aftershave reached my nose. "Oh, hey. You look... good." Good didn't even begin to describe how incredibly he filled out his cutoff denim shorts and pink tank.

He pushed from the wall. The air was alive between us. I should have stepped away then but I didn't, weak fool that I am.

"So do you," he murmured. "Sorry about the loss and all that."

"Thanks, it wasn't our time." How often had I said that now?

"Yeah, next year."

"For sure."

That was us done. Unless we started talking about the weather, then we'd covered the most relevant subjects, and I needed to get the hell away from Mason, his eyes, his laugh, and his damn dimple.

"You're leaving aren't you." There was no question there, just a statement, and I nodded.

"Uhm yeah, I think so. I'll leave the hijinks to you kids."

Even in the subdued lighting I saw him bristle. I was prepared for that, he always snapped at his brother and me when we called him a kid. This was familiar ground and led to tussles and head rubs and all the close physical things I needed to avoid.

"Yeah, so, bye." I stepped aside and moved past him, only he gripped my arm, and I was *not* prepared for that.

"We need to talk," he said and placed his other hand on my chest. I shook off his hold of my arm, but I didn't move away, lost in the heat in his eyes.

"I don't want to talk," I lied. *It's too dangerous. Don't talk to me, don't look at me, don't touch me.*

Chapter Four

Mason

I wish I knew what to do now. Becca had spent the last thirty minutes explaining how if I didn't talk to Xander today she was going to lock the two of us in a room until I faced up to how I was feeling.

I knew how I felt. I was in love with him, and I had been since I was fourteen.

And now I was stuck in a darkened hallway, a party just outside, *my brother right there with the rest*, and I was going for it. Putting everything out there, telling Xander how I felt, and handling the fallout.

"We have things to say to each other," I began and cleared my throat, the scent of his shampoo and the way I had to crane my neck to look up at him so familiar.

"I need to go, kid." He placed his hand over mine and gently removed it from where I was touching his chest.

Flirt with him. Becca was in my head again. Flirting. Okay, I could do that.

"I'm not a kid, Xander. I think you know that." Before I could second guess myself, I rose to my toes and pressed my lips to his, taking him by surprise as he reared back in shock.

For the longest moment, he stared at me, and then he raised a hand, cupping my face and rubbing his thumb on my cheekbone. I couldn't move, or take my eyes off him, wondering if the heat in them was mirrored in my own.

"Jesus," he muttered and in a smooth move, he pressed me back against the opposite wall and kissed me. Only this wasn't a soft, gentle touch. It was hunger and lust and need, and it was a clash of teeth and tongues. I scrambled to grip hard to any part of him I could get to, just for balance. He gentled the kiss, tilted his head, carded his hands through my hair, held me still, and I was done. I was not at all prepared for this kiss, and I don't think he could have been either. He groaned into the taste of it, nibbling at my lip then tangling my tongue with his, and his cock was hard against my belly. I wanted to be higher. I wanted to climb him so I could feel the rigid length of him pressing against mine, and I tried to move, but he held me still.

I gripped his ass, all hard muscles under shorts loose enough that I could slip my hands under to get my first touch of his skin, warm and smooth and everything I wanted. His touch roaming across my body, from shoulders to hip bones, resting them there for a second and then gripping me and lifting me up on my toes. I wanted his hands on me. I needed him to fall to his knees, suck me. I wanted to suck him… I wanted everything.

"Xander! Come and sort these fuckers out!"

Hearing my brother's voice broke us apart. Not by me,

I was clinging to Xander like a limpet, pathetically trying to hold on as he wrenched away, extricating himself from my hold and palming his cock.

"Coming!" he called, and I winced at the strength of his hockey game yell.

My brother cursed loudly. "Hurry the fuck up, dude!"

"One minute, asshole!" Xander called back.

We stood in silence staring at each other. "Xander?" I asked with caution.

"No." He took a step back, avoiding my hand as I reached for him. "What are we doing? No, what am I doing—this isn't happening. No."

He tugged his shirt down over his shorts, rubbed his face, and left. The sound of the door slamming behind him was the first moment I was even able to move, but it wasn't to follow him. Bypassing the hallway and heading through a door at the back, I stepped into my small apartment, shut and locked the door, then slid to the floor and buried my face in my hands.

I'd just fucked everything up.

EVEN TWO WEEKS LATER, WITH THE GIFT OF BLURRED memories, I couldn't deny the kiss had happened, and that I'd thrown myself at him. I'd tried denial but it didn't work, and it morphed slowly into anger. I still hadn't processed the fact that he'd shoved me away and told me no. Which led me straight onto the third stage of this shit fest. Bargaining. Last week I'd written out a text offering to meet and talk but realized it was a really bad idea in a world of bad ideas.

I didn't send the text, but at least I'd gotten my head around the fact that he'd called time on a kiss, as well, it seemed, as anything else. Closely linked to bargaining came more embarrassment, and at that point, I came up with a whole load of excuses not to go to Aruba. Then I slipped into a weird depression. It didn't happen overnight, it kind of crept up on me, and I didn't even really notice until I saw two empty Ben and Jerry's containers on my counter and realized I'd cleared them both in one day. Eli noticed though, which is why he stood in my room early this morning, staring down at me as I woke up, scaring the shit out of me, and brandishing my passport menacingly.

"No more excuses, we're going to Aruba!" he shouted down at me as I scrambled away and fell out of bed.

He wasn't going to let me mope about giving up my safe job, apparently. *If only he knew the real reason.*

And now I had to move on to acceptance. Lots of people have crushes, and not all of them work out. Hell, I used to imagine marrying Enrique Iglesias, watching the "Hero" video on repeat, pausing it when Enrique sang that he could take away my pain. The year Xander and Eli left for Boston was the year of Enrique. My reasoning was that if I concentrated on marrying not-gay Enrique then I wouldn't have to think about my unrequited crush on also-not-gay Xander. Problem solved.

I should have canceled this whole stupid party vacation thing that Eli wanted for Xander. I could have said I wanted to stay at home because I was busy. The idea of two weeks in Aruba, just me, Eli, and Xander had sounded like such a great idea when Eli had suggested it, but then, with Xander's big announcement and my own all-consuming feelings getting in the way, the idea had turned to shit. Eli had been the one to buy Xander the vacation as a thirtieth birthday gift, he just never mentioned that me and him would be turning up to help celebrate.

This was going to be so bad. But still I was here, in the car, heading for the airport next to Eli, ready to spring the surprise on an unsuspecting Xander, who was heading to Aruba thinking he was on his own.

I should have known something was wrong when Eli bypassed the main exit for Logan International Airport and instead headed out toward the private area reserved for chartered flights. In fact, I should have known this birthday vacation was going to go horribly wrong when Eli guilted me into still going. Apparently, my excuse that life was busy wasn't going to cut it, and the guilt and pressure was trademark Eli. He pointed out that I didn't have a job anymore, and I pointed out that this was the very reason I couldn't go because Becca and I were very busy with the new venture. Only Becca turned to us, all innocent, and said we couldn't do anything until contracts were signed on the new property, so hey, I should go to Aruba.

How did I get out of this vacation? I couldn't exactly, to be honest.

Yeah, sorry, big bro, but I sucked face with your best friend, and he rejected me, and he hates me, and my heart is freaking broken.

"You've gone past the airport." I sighed. Eli was a crap driver at the best of times.

"I hired a jet."

"For the two of us? You have more money than sense."
I wasn't shocked my stupid ass millionaire brother had
done something that ridiculous. He'd been in charge of
flights, and yeah, I'd imagined we'd be flying first class
but a private jet? That was either stupid or it was
something else altogether.

"We split the cost." He added his car to a line of flashy
cars a lot like his and killed the engine.

Wait? What? "What do you mean, *we* split the cost."

"The team." He spoke like that wasn't news to me, but
our birthday surprise with just the three of us had suddenly
become something different.

"All the team?" God help me if Xander was on this
fucking plane. Fourteen days since that kiss and I still
flushed scarlet thinking about the way I'd thrown myself at
the man and got off, every single night since, to the
memories of the kiss and the way he held me. Becca called
me an idiot for not demanding Xander stay, but I think
he'd made it very obvious that he didn't want to be with
me by his emphatic use of the word no. Something he'd
repeated three times if I recalled right.

I thought I'd have the flight to get my head around
seeing him. Hell, I'd decided I'd go into the small
bathroom to practice my nonchalance for when I saw
Xander again.

"Marquis, Renco, Dunny, and me."

Jeez. It was like a who's who of the single guys, all of
them prank-playing idiots.

"Oh, and Austin who is bringing his boyfriend with
him."

"Xander's not gonna like this—"

"He'll love it!" Eli enthused, but I didn't get a chance to argue any more when Eli spent at least five minutes explaining to the poor valet guy just how his sapphire blue F-Type should be placed carefully away from other cars, and that he'd taken a picture of the mileage just in case *people* decided to take it for a joy ride.

The valet and I exchanged looks, and I shook my head and rolled my eyes. Eli and his damn car had this weirdly symbiotic relationship, and both Xander and I teased him that he needed to get laid instead.

And there it was, my thoughts returning to Xander, and my face heating as a consequence, which I would've then had to blame on the warm Boston day if I was asked. The rejection still stung, the lust I swear I'd seen in his eyes had to be due to a lack of sex in his life, or maybe some unconscious reaction to losing against LA. Who knew what it was, but the embarrassment was real.

"Earth to Mason?" Eli poked me in the belly and pulled me from my woolgathering. "Bags?"

"Asshole," I grumped and pulled out my one small bag from the teeny tiny trunk. Then hoisted the rucksack that'd been on my lap all the way here, up and over my shoulder. "Travel light, he says. It's Aruba, he says. Let's have some brotherly bonding, he says! Just the three of us," I mumbled under my breath. "I could've stayed at home," I said louder.

"Stop moaning, you have the next two weeks off, and it's a free vacation for which you've created a detailed itinerary."

"Yeah, for three of us." *Two when I used a whole list of excuses I'd mentally listed.* "Not an entire team."

"You'll have fun with all the guys."

"Fuck you."

"Fuck you back, freeloader!" Eli grinned at me as if he didn't know it hurt to hear him call me that. I know I was lucky. Having my own place at my brother's house, with no rent or utilities to pay meant I'd saved a good amount of money to go toward the new venture with Becca. But yes, I knew I was freeloading. Still it was part of the brother code that I get my own dig in.

"It's not free when I have to put up with your face or you breaking in and staring down at me when I'm asleep," I groused.

"You'll enjoy the break, get out of your head, see the world."

"Whatever. It was bad enough when it was just us, but now you add jocks with no social skills." I tried to get the last word in, but of course, Eli wasn't going to let me.

"Think of the women in bikinis!" Eli pointed out and that earned him a smack upside his head, which he shrugged off as if it was nothing. Which it probably was, given he was used to landing on his head.

The jet was party central for the five hours it took to get to Aruba and land in Oranjestad. Mostly I joined in because what sane younger brother didn't like shooting the shit about pranks in the locker room, particularly ones involving Eli and focusing on his humiliation.

Austin and his boyfriend were a surprise, kind of cute and optimistic about their future. What I wouldn't have given to have fallen so deeply in love at their age. *I did. Only with Xander.*

I tuned out when the talk turned to sex, or hockey, or

when the mood dipped as the younger guys on the team talked about losing to LA. Then I put in my headphones, sat back in a luxurious seat with an ice cold Sprite, and thought back to my reaction at the thought he might be on the jet.

Horror? Was it that? Excitement? Embarrassment?

I turned up my music, settled even deeper in my seat, and closed my eyes.

I have to accept that I have no chance with Xander. I have to move on.

I can do this.

Chapter Five

Xander

GOD ABOVE BUT I LOVED FIRST CLASS.

Sure, it was a bit pricier—actually a *lot* pricier—but the privacy one was given was worth the extra cost. Solitary had been my middle name since that night at the party when Mason and I had locked lips. I'd shrugged off going out with Eli or hanging at his house for fear I'd run into Mason. Perhaps my middle name should be cowardly more so than solitary. Glancing out the window as my plane waited in line for takeoff, I drifted back to that night. *The* night as I'd taken to thinking of it. Everything had been fine then that kiss. Looking further back, I had to confess that I'd thought Mason'd carried a torch for me when we were younger. He threw off little clues. A shy look, a soft smile, the way he showed off in front of me. Of course, back then I'd been playing myself off as straight because I'd been unable to face myself.

But the kiss? It was like Renco in our loss with LA

when he'd expected the five hole and the shot had gone top shelf, it was unexpected and life changing and way out of my comfort zone.

The plane lurched forward another five feet. Sighing, I checked my belt and studied the tarmac. Yes, coward did seem to be the better choice for that middle name. My default was to pull back into my shell like a snapping turtle when things got uncomfortable. Case in point… me sitting here on a jet to Aruba to celebrate my upcoming birthday alone, courtesy of a birthday gift from Eli. No one other than my family and him knew where I was going or that I planned to be there for two weeks. Xander the Cowardly Turtle. Someone should write a children's book about me.

Look, kids, this is Xander. Xander is afraid to face himself or his feelings so he hides in his thick shell. I wonder what the fuck *is wrong with Xander, don't you?*

Okay, so maybe penning children's literature isn't for me. Still the point was a valid one. I was taking off for an island getaway to drown my sorrows about losing the Cup, my captain/dear friend/defensive partner talking of retiring, and my growing attraction for my best friend's younger brother. The rolling bar would get a good workout on this close to five hour flight. We had to get into the air first though. Departing Logan could be a nightmare at times. Sitting here with my thoughts was also unpleasant. Soul weary I closed my eyes, blocking out the airport and my fellow passengers to focus on finding inner peace. Meditation was something that I played with from time to time when I was exceptionally stressed. As a last resort sort of thing mostly, but over the past few weeks, I'd been seeking it out more and more. I no longer had hockey to take my mind off all those life worries, and I couldn't jog or lift weights on a packed 747, so introspection it had to be. Pulling out my earbuds, I plugged them into my phone and pulled up a beginner's meditation YouTube video I'd been using.

Listening to the sound of my breathing, focusing on the in and out, easing myself into that soft state of relaxation was working. The sounds of the other passengers talking began to fade away as the deep, relaxing voice of the narrator began to ease the tensions and worries piled up on my back. He spoke of finding a place in your mind to linger in. Somewhere warm and breezy, a beach perhaps or a woodland glen. Anywhere that brought solace and serenity. The plane began rolling, the seams of the tarmac a steady thump, thump, thump as I tried to dredge up a place where I felt whole and happy. Mason's face appeared.

"I'm not a kid, Xander. I think you know that."

His mouth had touched mine. What I said in reply, I couldn't recall, but instead of pushing him away or gently teasing him as I'd been doing for years, I moved into the kiss. Reveled in it, encouraged it, *wanted* it…

The man felt so good in my arms, so hard and strong. Perfectly crafted muscles and sharp edges, citrus aftershave or shampoo, the scrape of new whiskers, a stiff prick. No, Mason was certainly not a kid anymore. He was all man and for that short moment in time, we'd come together perfectly. The taste of him had faded, but I could still feel his hands on my ass and the way he'd lapped into my mouth. My body reacted now as it had then, my cock plumping, my hands yearning to touch, my heart hammering against my breastbone…

The jet began to pick up speed. My eyes flew open just as the front wheels left the ground. I felt the force of takeoff on my chest, or perhaps that pressure wasn't related to leaving the ground at all. Maybe it was the weight of craving something I knew I had no business craving. Cussing to myself, I yanked out the earbuds and watched Boston grow smaller and smaller as I shoved at my erection with the heel of my hand. So much for mental cleansing and mindful quietude. Guess it was going to take a few Jack Daniels on the rocks to align my radically misaligned chakras and restore harmony to my chaotic head.

WHEN WE TOUCHED DOWN, I'D FOUND MY MELLOW. IT had been with me the whole time… it just needed a little Tennessee whiskey to lure it out. The Sheltered Sands Resort had a shuttle waiting for me. A cheery man named Esmar was waiting for me with a big sign reading MR. XANDER and a bigger smile. He led me to baggage claim, found my bags, and then hustled me out into the warm tropical sun. I took a moment to enjoy the balmy breeze on my face as well as marvel at the palm trees swaying in the wind.

"Mr. Xander, we have to check in by four sharp," Esmar said, taking me by the elbow and leading me to the big blue Range Rover with the resort's logo on the doors. I grinned at the rainbow gulls over the lettering, my head buzzing with alcoholic happiness.

"I'm bisexual," I told Esmar. "These are my birds." I patted the logo lovingly.

The middle-aged man in the red shirt and khaki shorts chuckled. "Then you will love the Sheltered Sands, Mr. Xander. We're LGBT friendly and set up many fun activities for our gay, lesbian, and transgender guests. We have dances and parties, scuba diving excursions, and… not that way, Mr. Xander, this way. Yes, step up. Oops. Try again. There we go. Now sit down. Yes, let me buckle you in."

"I can buckle my own belt," I sniggered, slapping at his hands. "Watch me."

When the buckle snapped, I hooted in glee. Esmar nodded proudly, closed the door, and hurried around to the rear to throw my bags into the back. I inhaled and exhaled, the warm booze glow settling in nicely.

"Hey, Esmar," I asked when he climbed in and settled behind the steering wheel. "I feel glowed on. How many drinks did I have on the plane?"

"I'm not sure, Mr. Xander, but maybe a few?" He gave me a wink in the rearview. I liked him. He was funny and had a lovely Spinach accent. Wait. No. Not spinach. Spanish. I snorted and giggled behind my hand. When I had less of a whiskey glow, I wanted to sharpen my Papiamento skills so I could speak with the locals. I had a keen ear for languages and had studied and mastered several—mostly curse words from players I'd met. Still, I liked to show people that I was willing to put in the effort to learn how to communicate with them in their native tongue. Yes, most on the island spoke English, Dutch, or Spanish, but I wanted to go that step beyond. Just not right now obviously.

"Spinach," I sniggered softly.

The ride from the airport to the Sheltered Sands Resort took about twenty minutes. Esmar chatted the entire way, telling me about the sights to be seen during my stay.

"… beautiful beaches of course but there are so many other places to see. The Bubali Bird Sanctuary, the Butterfly Farm, and the Old Dutch Windmill. There is also the National Archaeological Museum close by. If you wish to go to any of those places, just call down and ask for Esmar. I will take you wherever you wish to go, Mr. Xander."

"Will do," I replied, the wind coming in the open windows was thick with the smell of the sea.

We pulled up in front of a magnificent high-rise resort dotted with palm trees. I inhaled the smell of salt water and held it as long as I could. Yes, oh yes, this place was going to work wonders for my mental health. Two full weeks of sun, surf, and sand would be the perfect way to put Mason Kingsley and his sensual lips back into the buddy box where he belonged. Then life would be smooth and normal again. I could stick my head out of my shell once the whole Mason situation was in hand. I freed myself from the seatbelt and exited the Rover, my gaze skipping up the massive resort's white walls.

"This place is even prettier in person than it was online," I told Esmar when he came up beside me with my bags.

"We think so too. Come now, we'll get you registered

and then maybe you can nap or go to the pool around back to wink at the pretty men."

Yes! Winking at pretty men was perfect. Once I found my room and took a tiny nap. Somehow I managed to sign in and get my room key. The staff were all lovely. A bellhop toted my bags for me while simultaneously keeping me from falling out of the elevator onto my face when we reached the eighth floor. He moved with grace and skill. He could be a hockey player. I told him so. He smiled widely, turned me around, and then herded me down a long corridor filled with tan walls, big plants in pots, and all kinds of people coming and going. Most in swimsuits or shorts and tops with walking shoes. Maybe they were going to the bird sanctuary or butterfly farm.

I made a mental note to go see the butterfly and bird places. The bellhop helped me scan my key card then gently maneuvered me into my suite. I gasped at the sight of my room. It was stunning. Wide open and airy. White and blues and tans ran through the draperies, carpeting, and bedding. I toed off my sneakers then raced to the sliding glass doors to gaze down on an Olympic-sized pool to the left and the ocean to the right. Oh the joys of having an end suite.

"Can I get you anything else?" the bellhop asked. I peeled my face from the glass, spun around, and shook my head.

"No, thank you. This is superb. I love it here. Wait! Don't leave." I shoved my hand into my front pocket, pulled out my phone and a wad of bills, and peeled a couple of fives off. "Here. This is for your help. I'm going to lay down for a bit now." I waved a hand at the big bed.

"Pleasant dreams, sir." He pocketed his tip, pulled the drapes closed for me, and then backed out of the room. I made a circle of the suite, taking in the door to the bathroom standing open then dove into the bed. The sheets were stiff and clean. They had a lingering aroma of citrus to them. It made me think of Mason and the lemon-lime taste of his mouth when we'd kissed. He must have had a Sprite to drink before he'd come to me. Mm, my body tingled at the thought of Mason coming to me again with a kiss on his mind. I buried my face into a fat pillow, closed my eyes, and dreamed of soft lips and summer loves.

I'd been asleep no longer than ten minutes when some asshole began hammering on my door. I was instantly mad. The jerk had interrupted a dream that included me, Mason, gentle winds, and sex on the beach. Not the vodka, cranberry juice, Schnapps, and orange juice version. I mean ball slapping hyena howling sex. Sand in delicate places. Crabs pinching your ass. Sunburn on your taint. That kind of sex. My dick was so hard it hurt. As did my damn head. I yelled something at the moron pounding on my door. It was a dirty word followed by several dirtier words. The asshole laughed and called to me to open the door.

I sat up, ran my hands through my hair and over my face, and then chanced a look at the big round clock on the wall. Eight p.m. No. That wasn't possible. I'd just laid down ten minutes ago. Oh fuck my head hurt. Badly. Jesus.

"Xander, open the damn door, dude!" Rubbing at my eyes with the tips of my fingers, my brain slowly picked up on the fact that the sphincter at my door knew my name and sounded a lot like Eli Kingsley. Like. A whole lot. I tried to shout back but had to take a second to scrape the foul barnacle-like crud from my tongue with my teeth. Why had I drunk so much on the plane? I hated being hungover. What had possessed me to indulge in so much—

Oh. Right. It had been a Kingsley. Only not the big lumbering dickwaffle making enough noise to wake the dead. It was the younger one. The one I'd just been pounding into the white sands while he passionately called my name over and over…

"Xander!"

Honest to fuck I was going to kill him, best friend or not. What the shit was he even doing here?! I got to my feet, head thumping, and staggered to the door. I whipped it open with vigor. There stood Eli. And right beside him? Mason who was backed by Dunny, Renco, and Marquis. My eyes, dry as they were, flared at the sight of them standing outside my door. Eli looked pleased as punch. Mason looked like he had a hedgehog crammed up his ass.

"What the *fucking hell* are you guys doing here?"

"Surprise, dude! We're staying here too!" Eli threw his arms around me. "Like we'd let you spend your thirtieth birthday all alone? You need your bros with you when you're officially over the hill. Group hug!"

I gawked at Mason then Eli reached for his baby brother and tugged him in for a three-way brotherly hug. That sinful citrus shampoo smell wafted off Mason as his nose was crushed into my clavicle. He stiffened. I tensed. Eli pounded on our backs as he yammered on about besties for life. He'd be singing a different tune if he'd seen what I'd been dreaming about doing to his little brother…

Chapter Six

Mason

I EASED OUT OF THE HUG, AWARE THAT IF I STAYED THIS close to Xander for a moment longer, then not even my tight cutoffs would be enough to control my burgeoning erection. He smelled terrible, a mix of stale air and alcohol, his beard was flat, his eyes were bloodshot, but I'd never seen anything as perfect as Xander staring at us as if we'd pissed in his Wheaties.

"The fuck?" Xander said for probably the third time. I think he'd lost the ability to speak.

"My man, Xand!" Dunny yelled and barreled into us, followed closely by Renco who attempted to drag Dunny off from all of us. Marquis just lingered in the hallway looking unsure of how he should insert himself into things being the new man on the team and all. "We're here to party!" Dunny added, just as loudly, and I winced at the way the blood drained from Xander's face. It could be a headache or the fuzziness of sleeping on his face which still showed crease marks from a pillow, but he was totally spaced-out and probably in shock.

"Party?" Xander murmured, weakly.

"Girls! Boys! Food! Drink! Swimming." I clapped a hand over Dunny's mouth to stop him from listing the supposed pluses in his extra loud booming voice, and he licked my palm, which made him snort a laugh and me cringe at not knowing where Dunny's tongue had been. Hell, we'd been in Aruba all of an hour, and he'd already kissed two people that I was aware of.

"Boundaries," Eli reminded Dunny and then shoved him off me. "Now fuck off and leave us alone."

Renco dragged Dunny away with a casual wave, his big beefy arm around Dunny's neck and through all of it, I stared at Xander's shocked expression because I could. Marquis gave us one of his regal nods then ambled along with the other two. Only the moment he turned back to Eli and me, I dropped my gaze and took a step back.

"I'll let Eli explain this one," I said with forced joviality. "Nothing to do with me."

As I walked down the corridor, I thought I heard Xander call my name, but I know that was wishful thinking. Anyway, whatever he said was lost in Eli shoving Xander back in his room and the door shutting.

At least I had my own room, and I headed down the stairs and back there immediately. I only had my own room because I'd written it on the plan. I certainly never wanted to share with my brother—I'd had enough of that growing up—and the room came with privacy and a stunning view over the ocean and the endless blue skies above. There was a bed built for giants, and since I was on the ground floor, beyond the billowing voile at the patio doors, there was a short path down to the ocean. In fact, the ocean was so close that the soft susurration of the waves filled every corner of my room. Taking an icy cold water from the mini-refrigerator I went outside and sat on a patio chair and soaked it all in until after an hour or so the stress began to shift.

The agenda I'd created with a lot of thought for what Xander and Eli would enjoy doing started tomorrow, so today was marked with the word arrival and nothing more. Only who knows what happened to the agenda now we had a big group of other hockey players hanging around. On the plus side, more people meant it would be easier for me to get out of going anywhere with Eli and Xander. That way I could avoid him and keep my emotions to myself.

I slid down in my chair, pushing my feet into the sand that started where my patio ended, and waved at Austin and Robbie as they passed by on the shoreline. I had some privacy here, with huge plants separating me from the patios of the rooms on either side, one Dunny's, and the other Eli's. I'd only booked three rooms, but without me knowing Eli had taken over this entire block of large airy rooms, fucker. The only upshot was that there would be no one to disturb the NHL stars in their down time, and me, by association. I closed my eyes and soaked up the diffused rays and tried not to focus on Xander being in one of the rooms above me.

Stop thinking about Xander.

"Hey."

Well shit. How can I try not to think about Xander when he was standing in front of me? I opened one eye to check, just in case it was someone else who sounded like Xander, but nope, I wasn't that lucky. His hair was wet, and his face finally clean of the playoff beard that had hidden his strong jaw and the cute dimples that popped when he smiled. Even showered and shaved he still looked rough, but that was probably due to lack of sleep and whatever booze he'd imbibed on the plane.

"Hey, Xander." *Don't stare at his pillow soft lips. Just don't.*

"Can we talk?" He winced as he spoke and rubbed at his temples. I screwed the cap back on the water and pitched the bottle at him.

"Hydrate," I ordered as he caught the bottle in one hand and stared at it as if I'd tossed him a grenade.

"I wasn't expecting all of this," he growled and frowned down at the bottle, savagely twisting the lid and then gulping mouthfuls of water until the entire thing was empty. What was it about hockey players and their need to do everything so damn dramatically? I guess I was lucky he didn't waste it by pouring it all over his face.

"Hang on, I'll get more water." I headed inside, and he followed me, tracking sand onto the thick blue carpet, belatedly realizing this and brushing his feet with his hand which did nothing more than scatter more of it around. I pulled out two waters but when I stood up again, he was right there in my space.

"I'm sorry," he blurted and then winced again. He was probably sporting a doozy of a headache, so I passed him a water and then went into the bathroom to find my personal bag, rummaging for the painkillers I knew were in there. "I am you know," he repeated from next to me, and I yelped in surprise. I never even heard him move. The contents of my bag exploded out and scattered on the marble surface. Toothbrush, paste, hair gel, Advil, lube, condoms. I stuffed it all back in, hoping to hell he wasn't going to comment on what he saw because then I'd have to be honest with him and tell him I intended to find a summer fling to work him out of my head.

"Here." I thrust two Advil at him, and he was as confused by that as he had been by the water. I pushed at his broad chest because he was blocking me in the bathroom, where the lube, condoms, and two man shower was, and my head couldn't handle all of that right now. "Sit the fuck down," I muttered. He stumbled back then kept going until his knees hit the bed, and he slumped onto it, rumpling the gorgeous dark blue covers.

"You weren't supposed to be here," he said then swallowed the tablets and drank more of the water, this time at a more sedate pace.

"I know. I guess you're pissed at Eli?"

He glanced up at me and gave a wry smile. "Nah, it was done with good intentions. I'm single. He's single, and hell the single guys on the team are here being all kinds of stupidly single, apart from Austin, who is being disgustingly cute. Hell, it's a single boys' vacation. I get it." He held out a hand toward me. "I just didn't want it."

I stepped closer and bumped his hand with mine because I thought he wanted me to sympathize, but instead of a casual touch, he closed his fingers around mine and held tight.

"Are you okay?" I asked as he tugged at me. I didn't move at first, but then he pulled a bit harder, and I took another step closer. He widened his legs and encouraged me to stand between them. My crotch was *this close* to his mouth, and there was no way in hell I was going to be able to laugh this off or pretend I didn't want him close to me. Xander was a casual toucher, the sort to hug me or lean on me, but this time it was different. He leaned forward and rested his forehead on my belly but didn't let go of my hand.

"I don't know how to do this," he muttered and every hair on my body stood on end at the absolute devastation in his voice.

"How to do what?" I rested my free hand on his head, idly stroking the soft mess of layers, and he sighed with his whole body.

"How to be me." He looked up briefly, his eyes dark with pain, and then he bowed his head.

I shook off his hold and crouched down in front of him. "Xander, look at me." I waited until he was staring right at me. "Are you still drunk?"

He closed his eyes then shook his head. "No, I promise, but I don't even feel right in my own skin. I don't know what comes next. How do I even be myself?"

God, how I wanted to grab him and kiss him and tell him that *I* was what came next, but I didn't. He'd been hiding who he was for so long that what he needed right now was a friend, not me demanding to know why he hadn't confided in me. I just wish I knew what to say because he was clearly hurting, and he needed this two week break without his damn team following him out here.

"I'll talk to Eli," I began but his eyes widened in horror.

"What? No!"

I lost my balance in shock at the overheated reaction and tumbled onto my ass on the carpet, which hurt because the carpet might be thick but landing on a discarded bottle was fucking *ouch*. I fished it out from under me though I didn't get up because I was very happy sitting on the floor, thank you very much.

"He'll understand if I explain it's all too much, maybe you could get a different hotel and—"

"I'm not letting the team down like that," he interrupted with what I call his stoic hockey expression— the one he'd used when he'd played three shifts on a broken ankle, and in another game pulled out a wobbly tooth and carried on playing. Heroic testosterone-driven idiots, all of them, my brother included.

"The *team* will understand if you wanted two weeks peace from them," I started, and he stood and crossed to the door, then back to me, and then to the door again. The room was big, but the space was too small for a six-two man to pace. I clambered up and blocked the pacing with a hand to his chest.

"Don't stop me," he growled, but I wasn't backing down from the guy, even if he had six inches and fifty pounds of pure muscle on me. I stared up at him with a level focus and in the end, he couldn't meet my gaze. He relaxed as he muttered something under his breath about little brothers.

"You said you wanted to talk." I poked his chest. "I'm guessing about what happened in the pool house and how you owe me an apology, right?" I said the last of it with a smile and expected him to chill the hell down and snark back at me, righting this weird situation we had going on.

"No."

"No, you're not going to apologize, or no you— oomph."

He grabbed me roughly and kissed me hard, softening the kiss after a few moments, then wrapped his big arms around me and held me tight, while licking along the seam of my lips. I was too shocked to even think about what was happening. I opened my mouth and welcomed him in, hard as a rock in my pants and scrabbling to get purchase on any part of his muscled body I could reach. I finally gripped the base of his T-shirt, pushed it up, and rested my hands on his lower back as he kissed me with thorough focus. I stepped back a little, he followed, one more step, and he stepped as well when I threw him off balance and only stopped when my back hit the wall, and I could think about whatever was happening here.

It's finally happening. He's kissing me.

We separated for a moment and I opened my mouth to ask him a "what the hell" question, and then he was on me again, pushing a beefy thigh between my legs and lifting me a little. I whimpered at the erotic beauty of being held hard between him and the wall. I pressed down against him, slipping my hands up and under his T-shirt, tracing the muscles of his back as much as I could.

He broke the kiss and buried his face in my neck. "I don't know how to be this," he said brokenly.

"Kiss me, Xan," I ordered, but something had changed, a subtle shift in the way he was standing, and how he held me. Where before it had been a hard and fiery passion, he was gentling, and I could have cried at the loss. I didn't want to be treated with kid gloves. I was desperate for him to touch me, and I wanted more soul-owning kisses.

"I can't." He moved away, and I was left hard and wanting with only the wall holding me up.

"Xander?"

His eyes widened comically, and he pressed a finger to his lips. "You're bleeding," he snapped, and I touched my lip and glanced down to see blood on my finger.

"It was one hell of a kiss." I tried for a smile, but he just looked horrified.

"I hurt you."

"No, you didn't, it happens."

He backed away then, shaking his head. "Eli could have walked in, he could have... he'll kill me." His voice cracked.

"Xan... "

"I'm too rough. I don't know how to... "

He wasn't too rough, rather he was strong and caring, and he held me absolutely still when he kissed me. He could probably lift me up, and God... Xander was every one of my dreams all wrapped up in sex. "Wait!"

He wasn't waiting. He was leaving but at the last minute he turned to face me, half in and half out the door to the patio. "I can't use you for sex!" he whispered loudly then vanished, leaving nothing except me with my waning erection and the absolute certainty that I didn't understand anything of what just happened.

Xander holding me up like that, his big hard body, hot as hell, stronger than... I ran out of superlatives for those kisses. I wished he *would* use me for sex because if we got sex into the equation, then I could show him I wanted him in a million small ways, and then he'd fall headlong in love with me, and we'd be forever.

Sex was good.

I needed to get him in my bed. Stat.

Chapter Seven

Xander

THE NEXT MORNING, REALITY HIT ME WITH A sledgehammer.

"What the actual, ever-loving fuck, Xander?" I asked my pitiful reflection in the steamy mirror of my luxury accommodations. Baggy-eyed, hungover Xander just stood there looking baggy-eyed and hungover. The loser. "Hey, ass wipe, I'm talking to you. What the hell possessed you? Kissing Mason. *Honestly?* Clinging to him, begging him to love you?" I poked my mirror image in one of his bloodshot eyes because he fucking deserved it. "Asshole."

I ran my fingers through my wet hair. Fuck a comb. Did I even pack a comb? Yes, of course. It was somewhere. In my small personal bag which was... who fucking knew?

Padding out into the suite, naked, I unzipped my suitcase and pulled out some swim trunks. Plain blue trunks. No racing stripes or flames. Just plain blue trunks. The kind that did not attract attention because Xander Holden was all about staying under the radar. Or had been. No, still was. Had to be. Needed to be cool. Collected. A model queer man.

"The world is watching," I muttered to myself as I stepped into my trunks. And that I knew to be true. Hell, even after all the time had passed for Brady's brother, the press still kept a sharp eye on Ten and Jared. Every little thing they did was newsworthy.

First bi player in NHL marries! First bi player in NHL adopts a baby! First bi player in NHL takes out the trash!

It was really insane, but it was the reality of being out. A reality I'd hoped to avoid until after I'd retired but que será, será.

No, dumbass, that's a Doris Day song. You mean c'est la vie.

"Same thing now be quiet," I told my head so it would shut the fuck up. It was talking too loudly. I dug into my personal bag, used my deodorant and slid my feet into a pair of ratty sandals. I'd packed for comfort not style. This was supposed to be fourteen days of rest and relaxation not two weeks of stress and sexual frustration. Putting on some shades and pulling on a short-sleeved shirt, I shuffled out the door with the intent of finding food and spending what remained of the day napping beside the ocean.

I shuffled around the lobby until I found signs telling me where to go. Seemed they had a buffet on the Pelican Bay Overlook. Cool. I followed a newlywed couple who appeared to be incredibly hungry given they were feasting on each other like vampires, but they ended up going to the elevators which I had just exited. Mind muzzy, I finally found a bellhop and he led me to the Pelican Bay Overlook which was just what it claimed to be. An overlook. Actually, it was a breezy, open-air porch that led to the whispering sands and sapphire sea. I took a minute to appreciate the beauty of the swaying palms and gentle ocean breezes then I got in line for grub.

I filled up on fruit and soft rolls then with my plate in hand, I glanced around for the other guys. I found Dunny right off, the mountain man was hard to miss. It was hard to overlook Sasquatch snoring away on a lounger with a copy of *Great Expectations* resting on his hairy chest. How the man could enjoy those dry old classics as he did I would never understand. Next to the man snoozing under Dickens was Marquis looking like he'd stepped out of a GQ beachside shoot. Plum trunks with a matching gauzy cover up, dark shades, and a slim gold watch—Rolex I was sure—and trendy white sandals.

"Gentlemen," I grunted as I took the lounge chair between them. Dunny snorted and sat up, his book sliding to his lap. Marquis gave me a scathing look over the top of his designer sunglasses.

"Not to be rude but you look like something the cat threw up," Marquis kindly pointed out.

"I think he looks okay," Dunny tossed out as he futzed around trying to find his page.

Marquis gave Dunny a long look. Then he glanced at me. Fine, I did look like shit. I knew it.

"I drank too much on the plane," I said as I placed my

platter of food on my thigh. "As soon as I get some nutrition into me, I'll be fine."

"It's going to take more than some fruit chunks to fix your look," Marquis dryly commented.

I ignored him. "Where's Eli and Renco?" I asked between bites just to divert the conversation from my ill-kempt appearance.

"Napping. We're supposed to meet up in the lobby later for an ATV guided tour of the western beach," Dunny interjected, his book now open once again.

"Great," I mumbled. Just what my head needed. Several hours on a four-wheeler bouncing and bounding over sand dunes. Why couldn't we just have an early dinner and some TV in our rooms?

Xander, holy hell you sound like your father when you took the folks to Hawaii! Dude, you're not even thirty yet. Live a little.

Ugh. Inner me was right. I *did* sound like my father. It was starting already and—

"Dayum," Marquis said. I glanced his way to see what had grabbed his attention, a skewer rising to my mouth when I spied Mason making his entrance. My kebob clattered back to my plate as my dick sprang to life instantly. I blinked stupidly at the man as he made his way to us in pink swim trunks that left little to the imagination. I mean his sizeable package was right there and covered with tiny bubblegum-colored flamingoes.

"I always loved this line. 'Love her! Love her! Love her! If she favors you, love her. If she wounds you'—holy hell." Dunny snapped his book shut and reached up to tidy his flowing brown beard. No one grew a playoff beard like

Dunny. My scruffy thing was pale in comparison. "Is that a sock in his swimsuit or is he just glad to see us?"

I had to swallow several times to empty my mouth of drool. Fuck but Mason was stunning. He had the lithe build of a swimmer or gymnast, although I knew he was neither. My gaze roamed over all that sweet flesh as he flip-flopped his way to us. I could not look away. My balls ached, and my cock was tipping up my plate.

"Hey there you are. Just heading to the water for a bit. Make sure you're all in the lobby by four for the ATV ride. It'll be awesome! Okay, bye!" Mason smiled down at us. I was blinded by his grin. Then he turned and made his way to the stairs leading to the warm sands. My God his ass was a thing of divine beauty. Tight and high, cradled in soft pink nylon and Lycra, his tiny buttocks bounced just a bit as he walked. Fuck. That ass. I wanted it now. Right now. On my plate next to the chunks of melon and pineapple.

"Well, that was quite the suit," Marquis finally said. I nodded dully hoping my erection wouldn't dump my food. "Pink looks good on him."

"I love summer," Dunny chuckled. "Get to see all the fine young bods." He eyeballed two girls who sashayed past. For a man who looked like a wild-eyed hermit freshly arrived from the mountain top, he certainly got enough action. Dunny winked at the girls. They giggled and waggled fingers back. "And that's my cue to put Pip and Estella aside for a bit. See you boys in the lobby!"

Dunny pushed to his enormous feet and pattered off after the women, his book under his beefy arm. I cleared my throat while trying to look nonplussed.

"Think those two are into Dickens?" I asked then glanced at Marquis. He was assessing me like a microbe on a slide over the top of those damn shades of his. "What?"

"Nothing. Just making sure you're okay. You stopped breathing when Mason was here."

I flipped off my teammate. He snickered softly. I'd leave in a huff of righteous indignation, but my dick was too hard. So, I had to sit there, hard as a post, chewing cold chicken, while Marquis made snide comments. This birthday trip was going to be the fucking death of me.

I WAS WRONG.

It wasn't the trip that was going to put me in the cold, cold ground. It was Mason. And miserable ass four-wheelers.

Whoever had come up with this idea needed to be shot in the kneecap. Yes, the beaches were beautiful. And yes, the other guys seemed to be having a blast roaring along like juveniles hooting and hollering as they bounded over dunes. I was not enjoying the outing. Riding an ATV with a perpetual hard-on was shitty. My dick was just not willing to go down with Mason right there, everywhere, in my face with his face. His beautiful, sun-kissed face.

Fuck.

I shifted on my seat, never so glad to see a damn restaurant as I was the one we were riding up to. The meal at JOX DOT was not part of the package plan with the ATV company, but it was a common ending spot for tourists. The guides shook our hands, pocketed the tips we all slipped them, and began loading the four-wheelers onto long metal trailers.

My ass and balls were still vibrating from the steady hum of the engine between my thighs. Hopefully, now that I was off the damn machine my cock would deflate. Mason was, it seemed, my personal Viagra. I needed to get some space between us before my balls burst, or I did something as stupid as kissing on him. Again. That required an apology, I was sure. I had little knowledge of dating a man since I'd always been the one seeking out a dirty BJ in an even dirtier bathroom stall, but I was sure kissing and groping and sniveling without consent was a no-no.

"Dude, this is your birthday trip. You've *got* to lighten up!" Eli said as he dropped an arm around my shoulders and led me into JOX DOT for dinner. The eatery was packed but we had a couple of reservations that could be expanded if we squeezed together, thanks to Mason who, I'd learned, had set up our itineraries for the next two weeks. "Maybe you can find a guy at the bar?"

I glanced around the nicely decorated restaurant, done up in shades of blue and gray, to the bar and along the far wall. Mason was leaning over the bar, up on his tiptoes, talking to the bartender, a handsome dark-skinned man. My gaze landed on his ass. The shorts he had on were stretched tight across those two orbs. My dick twitched. I hurried to pull down my Hawaiian shirt over the bulge.

"Yeah maybe," I mumbled.

Mason joined us at our table, smiling and windblown, his cheeks pink from the sun. "The bartender, whose name is Malachi, will keep us set up with pink mojitos."

Pink. Damn it. My mind raced back to Mason in those sinful trunks. "I love those!" Renco announced with a rare smile. Our goalie was always so… withdrawn. Tense. As if he moved around under a perpetual fear of a piano falling on him. It was nice to see him relaxing a bit. We feasted on tuna tartar, rock lobster, and spicy vegetables. Key lime tartlets for dessert served with strong coffee. And throughout the meal pink mojitos were flowing. I didn't even like pink mojitos, but I sucked them down just to please Mason. Seemed I would do just about anything to please Mason which was bad. Eli would hate me if I pleased Mason the way I wanted to please him. Loving Mason would be so sweet, so sizzling hot, so wet and slick and—

"… had a fucking seagull in my face!" Dunny roared in glee, snapping me back to the table with a jolt.

"You should have been paying attention to the road and not that hot dude surfing," Marquis tossed out around the straw of his mojito. I looked around and came up one person short. My gaze flew around the eatery until it landed on Mason back at the bar. Up on his tiny toes, whispering to Malachi, he of the thick biceps and dreads. Fuck. Were they flirting? I stood up like a shot, my only thought was bulling my way to the bar and slinging Mason over my shoulder in true Cro-Magnon style.

"You leaving?" Eli asked lazily, his blood full of white rum just like mine was.

"Yeah, I'm done." I twisted around so as not to see Mason making eyes at Mr. Body Beautiful behind the bar. If kissing on him were a big negative then toting him out of this restaurant in a fireman carry was totally unacceptable. "I never fully recovered from the overindulgence on the plane."

"Lightweight," Eli said, blinked, and then snorted at himself. "Man, I had too many homitos."

"That's what Xan said," Marquis hooted. Renco did a fine spit take of pink liquid all over the table. Dunny rolled out of his seat to the floor howling with laughter.

Yep, vacation with the Rebels was in full swing. And to think I had dreams of two weeks of solitude and peaceful reflection all planned out. Instead of leaving by myself so I could brood over Mason, we all decided to go at once. Eli was easily seven sheets to the wind instead of the customary three. The only good thing about everyone heading out at once was that Mason had to leave his hot bartender flirt behind. Not that I cared whom he flirted with.

Liar, liar, entire wardrobe on fire.

Fine, okay, I cared. A little. Because he was like a younger brother to me, and I didn't want to see him get hurt by some summer romance.

Someone needs to get the pitchfork out because the bullshit is piling up fast.

My inner voice got really shady when he had a snootful of white gin it seemed. We called for a car and of course when it showed up it was a freaking compact thing. Which meant we had to cram five hockey players and Mason into the back seat. Having Mason wiggle onto my lap was so not good. I'd have much rather had Dunny on my thighs, or Marquis, or Renco. Hell, even Eli. But no, Mason made sure his ass was on my lap. I closed my eyes and let my head drop back, with Dunny's sharp elbow in my side, and tried to block out the scent of Mason's aftershave.

"Sit still," I hissed at Mason when he would wriggle.

"Sorry," he replied then commenced to wriggle. My poor dick was like a fire poker inside my shorts. He had to feel it pressed against his hip. Was he *trying* to drive me insane? "This was fun. Tomorrow we're going snorkeling then heading to this hip dance club. The catamaran will be ready at the dock for us at nine so everyone be at the lobby by eight."

I groaned. Not at the early wake up time. I was always up early to run or workout. My moan was caused by the knowledge that I'd be on a fucking catamaran with Mason. Who would probably wear his pink flamingo little bitty bikini bottom.

"Don't you like snorkeling?" Mason asked as the others talked animatedly about the trip tomorrow.

"I like it fine. Just fine," I said through gritted teeth. "I'm just sore from the ATV banging my ass."

Mason leaned in close, his lips brushing my ear. "I rather enjoy something banging my ass."

I nearly came in my shorts. The drive to the hotel took four thousand years. I'd never been so glad to shove my best friend at his brother and bolt to my room. I was barely in the door when I had my cock free. Shoulder blades pressed to the doorjamb, I fisted my dick and started jerking. All it took was for me to dredge up one of a thousand mental images of Mason. The one where he dropped to his knees to swallow my cock worked well. Too well. I came like a Clydesdale, coating my hand, cum dripping off to the carpet, my lungs working like bellows.

When I could breathe normally, I glanced down at my hand then the spunk soaking into the rich carpeting. What a weak man I was. I'd do better putting distance between myself and Mason tomorrow now that I'd gotten off. There was plenty of space on a catamaran.

I was so fucking doomed.

Chapter Eight

Mason

I WAS UP AND OUT OF MY ROOM AT FIVE HOPING THAT THE hotel shop would be open for early morning coffee seekers and that there would be no hockey players wandering around looking for the gym. Yesterday's plan had worked perfectly—the pink swimming trunks were exactly what I'd had in mind in my devious scheme to get Xander to look past all the reasons why kissing me was a bad idea. I'd packed the fact that Eli would kill him into a box marked "not if we hook up on the sly" and added to it all my own worries about why I was even doing this in the first place.

The moment he leaned his forehead on my stomach as if I was the only thing holding him up, I knew.

He *could* love me.

It wouldn't take much for me to show him that I could keep secrets as much as the next guy and that he could embrace his sexuality with my help.

I could help him realize that it was possible to love *me*.

I wasn't above the devious means to get him to crack because that kiss had been explosive, and he'd said he was too rough and that he couldn't use me for sex. I beg to differ. He wasn't rough, he was strong and persuasive and hard, and he could use me for sex all he wanted.

It will just be sex. I can leave my heart at the door.
Liar.

The shop was open, the short woman behind the counter tracking me as I went straight for the rack of swimsuits at the back. Yesterday's bottoms had a matching pair in yellow, with tiny cartoon suns on them, and I needed all the ammunition I could get in my plan to pull Xander. I picked them up, plus a muscle T in the same orange as the suns, then added matching yellow sunglasses. With extra sunscreen, backup condoms because a man can never have enough of those, and more lube *just in* case, I paid for it all and refused to rise to the smirk on the cashier's face.

"Have a *good* day," she said straight faced, and I channeled my inner child by winking at her.

"I intend to."

I deliberately added a sashay as I left the shop and walked straight into a hard chest. Hands steadied me, and I stared right into the bemused expression of one Xander Holden.

"My bad," I murmured, relishing the feel of him holding me and hoping that he wouldn't let me go.

"You're up early." He released me and stepped away. I don't think he really needed an answer but there was no way I was letting him leave.

"This isn't early," I lied. "Up until I resigned, I was commuting, working nine to five, which let's face it's never just those hours, plus trying to set up a brand-new company with Becca in my limited down time, *plus* organizing this vacation which my brother has then gone and messed up. Whatever. I've gotten used to getting up at five just to fit it all in." I really needed to stop talking because I could see him taking another physical step back from me.

He glanced past me at the shop. "You're shopping." Oh boy, he was a man of few words this morning. I saw shadows bruising his eyes, but he looked a hell of a lot better than he had yesterday, which was a step in the right direction.

"I needed toothpaste," I lied, again, when he glanced from me to the bag and up again. "You ready for the catamaran adventure?" I asked and closed the distance between us in the empty hotel lobby. "I know *I* am. Do you like yellow?" The last I whispered close to his ear, and he yelped. No joke, he seriously let out this surprised noise that I wouldn't expect from such a big bad hockey D-man.

"Yellow?" This time he backed away, and I let him move out of touching range, watching him with no small amount of regret when he couldn't quite meet my gaze. Part of this plan to show Xander that he could love me was to get him to take that first step and kiss me again, but all the barriers he had in the way were insurmountable this morning it seemed.

"Well, I had pink swim trunks yesterday. Today they're yellow."

He turned sharply and stalked away. I felt a twinge of

worry at pushing him but had no time to think about it because Eli appeared in the lobby, looking a hundred times hungover, and when he saw me, he held up a hand to indicate he didn't want any shit from me.

But that's what little brothers are put on this planet for.

"N'awwww, are you feeling poorly? You want me to kiss it better?"

"Fuck off," he growled and stepped to the right to get around me, only I knew the dance, and I pretended to go the same way. He might be fast on the ice, but I was faster on the carpet, and he knew it, so after a couple more steps he just stopped trying to get past me all together and put his hands on his hips. "What?"

"Nothing." I blinked at him with my best innocent expression, my mind working overtime as to how I was going to take this first step at sowing the seed in Eli's brain that Xander needed someone like me in his life. "Well, it's Xander." I leaned in, and I saw the moment his pissed expression cleared.

"I'm meeting him for breakfast, is he okay?"

"I'm worried about him since the big reveal. You know what it was like for me."

A shadow passed over Eli's expression, and I knew I had to be serious. I'd only just come out to our parents before they were taken from us in a car accident. They'd been one hundred percent supportive, but I'd been kind of lost for the longest time, and it had been Eli who'd hugged me and told me that he'd always have my back.

"Shit, has something happened? He was a mess after the flight. Do I need to talk to him? I don't get why he didn't tell me."

"If you thought it would help, I could probably talk to him."

"Okay, yeah, good idea."

"But I think he's avoiding me?"

Eli frowned, the last thing he would want is for his brother and his best friend to be at odds. "Shit, really? Okay, I'm on it."

I grinned at my brother and then bypassed him and left with a wave. I'd played my brother, pulled at emotions that were a mix of guilt and sadness, and felt a tug of guilt.

But one way or another I would help Xander.

"... SHALLOW WATER AND SANDY BOTTOMS. ARASHI Beach has small colorful fish, but you might spot a few larger ones in between. You'll see a lot of palometas near the shore as well as cute bottom feeders. There's hard coral about fifty meters out, so you may want to make your way over there." Lucas, snorkeling expert and catamaran owner, was at the side of the boat, having just finished the instructions and explaining what we might see. "So, having said that, if you could pair off."

I noticed that Eli immediately stepped closer to Dunny, which left Xander with me. I'm not sure anyone else would have noticed but step two in the great plan had worked so well that poor Xander hadn't known what hit him. From the moment we left the hotel, Eli had been encouraging Xander and me together, and at first, Xander hadn't really noticed. Only when Eli did some creative shuffling so that Xander and I ended up sitting next to each other on the jetty, something clicked, and I watched Xander as his eyes narrowed.

"What the fuck is your idiot brother doing?" he asked me through gritted teeth.

I patted his arm. "I thought you'd like to talk things through," I said with complete innocence. "And Eli thinks because I've been through all of this… " I waved between us.

"Through what?" Then his eyes were comically wide, but my chest hollowed at the fear in them, and for a brief moment, my scheme to get him to talk looked like a really shit one when he lowered his voice. "I don't need your advice."

"I know that." We were the last ones on the boat now, and Lucas was watching us curiously. "I just thought you'd like to talk to me about the kiss."

"Fuck no. I hurt you. I split your lip. It's not right."

"You didn't hurt me—"

"I don't know how to… " He ran a hand through his hair in exasperation. "I won't hurt you."

Before I got a chance to react, he went to the side of the boat and sat on the edge then without a backward look he eased himself into the ocean, and I followed him as quickly as I could. He hadn't hurt me, not in the way he thought he had, but there was so much trapped inside him as if he wasn't comfortable in his own skin, and I wanted to help.

Correction, I wanted him to fall in love with me.

I swam toward him and we snorkeled for ages, only stopping when it was time to get to the beach and eat lunch. I refused to feel hurt that Xander chose to sit as far away from me as possible when we were eating, sitting with his back to me, chatting with Dunny. Suddenly my stupid plan to wow him with new yellow swim trunks, to force him to look at me, seemed the worst one on the planet because the trunks were very small and the blood supply was being cut off. Idiot.

Getting him into bed with me to get him to admit how he felt was a shit thing to do, and this wasn't a game. Back on the boat he deliberately sat on a seat next to a huge cooler, which meant there was no room for anyone to sit next to him, and when he glanced over at me and caught my gaze, he immediately stared back at his feet. Dunny was telling some story about the night they did something with a puck and a stick that was, in his words, amazing, and I pretended to listen, but in actual fact, I was checking on Xander and hoping my new yellow sunglasses would hide my stare.

He had his head tilted back, leaning on his elbows, eyes closed, soaking up the sun, and all I wanted to do was go over and hug him and tell him everything would be okay. I caught Eli glancing over at him as well, and when he looked back he was frowning. I wish I hadn't put that worry into my brother's head this morning. Fuck, I wish I'd thought about all of this a bit more.

We headed back to the hotel, and as soon as sneakers hit the ground he was gone. He didn't answer my knock on his door, even if I called his name as loud as I dared to. I tried his cell, sent him a message, but there wasn't even a sign that he was online.

I'd fucked up.

Getting ready to go to the club was an exercise in

pulling my shit together. There was nothing I liked more than dancing, and cocktails, and then more dancing, and I'd put Gusto Night Club on the list, not because it was a gay club, but because it was apparently the best on the island. I didn't have any qualms about taking my brother and Xander there, but was it the best place for Xander right now, and would the rest of the guys be cool with…

"Stop overthinking," I told my reflection and went back to concentrating on getting ready. I nixed gelling my hair, letting it fall in soft layers, and applied smoky eyeliner with a practiced hand, with just the tiniest bit of lip gloss. Pulled on fitted pants and a loose white shirt that I left half unbuttoned. I met the guys in the lobby, the rest of them dressed to the nines, even Dunny who had done something cool with his hair so it was tamed. I immediately sought out Xander and the breath caught in my throat.

He wore dark dress pants, hugging his thick thighs, and the shirt he wore I recognized from the shop here, a pale flowery loose fitting cover that was almost see-through in bright light. I could see every line of him, and I know it wasn't deliberate—how could it be—but the way he was made just left me breathless. I've never seen anyone as beautiful as Xander Holden, and all I wanted to do was have the right to go up to him and kiss him hello. Maybe some of my lip gloss would slide off onto his lips and…

"Are you actually going to move, dickwad?" Eli shoved me, and my fantasies went sideways as much as I did.

"Get off me." I shoved him back, and we tussled in our brotherly way until we reached the van. There was a seat next to Xander at the back, and Eli gestured for me to sit there. I had things I wanted to explain to Xander, and maybe I could say them if I was there, so I buckled up and waited until the engine started. Only it was too quiet. So I said nothing serious at all.

"You having a good time?" I half whispered, leaning into him so I could get close. He shuffled away from me, but he did at least look at me.

"It's great," he said after a moment's pause, and that was all the conversation we had until we got to the club.

The club was noisy and chaotic and there was no chance to talk at all. Xander didn't dance, but he did sway by the bar, so it was up to me and Dunny to wow the dance floor. For a big man, Dunny was actually a smooth mover, and he even threw in a few gyrations that were way too sexy for him to stay on his own for long. Surrounded by people I soon lost him in his adoring crowd, so I found a quieter space and let the music consume me. Sinking into my happy place, I ignored the press of bodies and rocked out to classic seventies and eighties big-hair bands, reaching the pinnacle when "Dancing Queen" echoed over the sound system. My favorite dance song. I let out a yelp of happiness and joined in with a group of girls on a bachelorette party as we danced and lip-synced the whole thing, only stopping when some guys joined us, and I felt ready to move on from grasping hands and drunk smiles.

Back at the bar I didn't see Xander at first then spotted him at the back in the shadows, sipping a cocktail and looking as if he'd rather be anywhere than here. I was on a high from dancing, and maybe one or two cocktails, and crawled over Eli's lap to reach Xander, sliding into the seat next to him as Eli turned back to Marquis and leaned in to talk to him.

"What's up, Xan?" I took his cocktail and sipped it, turned out it was all fruit and not an ounce of alcohol in sight.

"You," Xander muttered. "What in god's name was all that?"

At first, I didn't understand the question, instead I searched his expression for context. He seemed pissed, frustrated; his eyes dark with some emotion I couldn't understand.

"What?"

He waved at the dance floor. "That."

"That?" I was confused, and then it hit me. "You mean dancing?"

"That wasn't dancing, that was fucking with your clothes on." He ground out the words, bitterness and derision in every syllable, and it hurt. What was wrong with dancing out there with everyone else, it didn't mean anything, it was *just dancing*.

"Huh?"

"I'm surprised you didn't end up kissing some random guy." Now he sounded hurt as if I'd done something terrible, and I didn't understand any of it. Until it occurred to me that he might be jealous, and that gave me a tiny thrill.

"I don't want to kiss anyone else." I leaned in even closer, and to anyone looking it would just seem as if we were talking in a noisy club. They wouldn't know that just being this close to Xander had me so tied up in knots I couldn't think. "I want to kiss you."

"It's not going to happen."

"Why?"

"Because… " His eyes narrowed, and his gaze dropped to my lips, and unconsciously I wet them, expecting him to kiss me right here in the crowded club in front of everyone. Instead, he stood up and made his way around the side of the table. "I'm out of here," he announced. Eli and Dunny both stood to go with him.

Eli looked back at me. "Are you coming?" he mouthed. It was one a.m. The music was hot, the dancing still *right* there, but Xander was going back to the hotel, and fuck if all my enthusiasm for dancing had vanished.

I climbed into the van. Eli sat next to Xander, and I was paired with Dunny who was buzzing and telling a story about a chicken and a waterpark. Marquis was filling our ears with some minor celebrity sighting he'd made at the club. God knows who because I wasn't listening.

Something had shifted in me today. I'd decided I didn't want to play games with Xander, but he was shutting down, and maybe it was time to give him space and let him come to me. Maybe the two of us together was a lost cause. He was bi, and I was gay, but that didn't mean we were going to be queer together or that he'd fall in love with me as hard as I loved him.

I had to be realistic and think that maybe I wanted something I could *never* have.

Chapter Nine

Xander

WHEN I AWOKE FOUR DAYS AFTER THE ILL-FATED catamaran outing, I realized I had only eighteen hours left until I was thirty.

Rolling over in my bed to watch the sun flickering through dancing palm fronds it struck me that I'd done little in my life. Perhaps struck wasn't the correct word. Struck would indicate that I'd been caught unaware. I'd not been. It had been niggling at me for some time that my life was nothing but hockey. Part of that was because I loved the game, and it demanded dedication which I freely gave. The other part of that sad scenario was due to the fact that I'd been living a life of self-imprisonment.

I sat up, dropped my feet to the floor, and rested my elbows to my knees as my gaze lingered on the tropical paradise on the other side of the window. It was quite the metaphor for my life up until now, wasn't it? I wanted more out of life than just hockey that much I knew. And now I could have it. I was out. There was no reason to hide behind the glass, brow to the pane, and let the world move on without me.

I stood then padded to the sliding door. Hands resting on top of my head my gaze touched on the white sands and the soft waves rolling in. All I had to do was open the door and step out into the breeze and embrace what life was offering. Would that include Mason? *Should* it include Mason? It was obvious that we were insanely attracted to each other. He'd made it clear he had feelings for me. God knows I yearned for him. But were yearnings and feelings enough to jeopardize a lifelong friendship? That was the hang-up. Well, one of many. Seemed I was a man of *many* hang-ups. I unlocked the door and threw it open. The cries of gulls and the earthy rhythm of the waves blew over my face. I breathed it all in, over and over, deep yogic breaths that expanded my chest. The sun was pink and new. Pink. God those swim trunks of Mason's…

Shaking a bit from the rush of want that washed over me, I took a few steps, mindful of the fact that I was in my underwear and others might see me, and simply was. There had been little time to spend reflecting. Mason had done one hell of a job setting up this trip. Every day we'd done something fun. Snorkeling, deep-sea fishing, parasailing, visiting natural pools where flamingoes dallied in the tidal waters, sunset sailing trips, horseback rides through Arikok National Park. Today was a trip to a butterfly farm. Mason hadn't missed a thing, and we still had a week to go. Tomorrow would be a day spent drinking with the boys. As much as I loved my friends, I was growing weary of being on the go.

Maybe I could sneak away tomorrow and just soak up the knowledge that I was now thirty years old with no plan for life other than playing a game that paid me embarrassingly well. Did I want to marry? Yes, God yes. Have kids? Yes, at least two. Buy a house for the kids as well as a dog and a cat? Totally. Did I have the balls to go after all of that? Maybe? It was odd being out. Good odd, obviously, even though the way I'd been shoved into outing myself had been shitty. Still, now that the brouhaha had died down a bit I would be able to be me. Xander. A single man looking for love without limits. Mason appeared in my mind's eye as he always did when I let my guard down. Pursuing him would be a massive case of looking for love in all the *incredibly* wrong places. Johnny Lee knew from whence he sang.

I gave the dawn light a bow of thanks and went to the gym for a run on the treadmill. The early hour meant I was the only person there which suited me fine. I was feeling introspective today. Probably because my twenties were going to be nothing but memories soon. I hit the run hard, pounding away at top speed with some raging metal throbbing through my earbuds. Afterward, I thought about hitting the steam room but opted to skip it. I showered back in my room, dressed for comfort, slipped into the hotel dining room for a buffet breakfast, and was just sitting down to my overflowing platter of eggs and bacon when a tingle raced up my spine. I glanced at the doors and there was Mason. I wasn't sure what it said about me that I sensed the man now before I even saw him. Something lame and pitiful I was sure.

He spied me and gave me a wobbly smile. He'd been

subdued the past few days. No more skintight trunks—more was the pity—and less flirtation. His clothing was still trendy and colorful, but he wasn't working his sex appeal as he had before. It was a relief… mostly.

"Morning," he said then eyed the buffet. "I need caffeine." He placed a 35 millimeter camera on the table beside the salt and pepper shaker. That was new.

"Go for it." I watched him move around the steamtable, taking a little of this and a bit of that. He'd never been a big eater, not like Eli and me. Which was probably how he stayed so lithe. When he returned to the table, I saw he had mostly fruit, a cup of yogurt, and a bagel slathered with cream cheese. And here I was inhaling cheesy eggs and smoky pig meat.

"Have you seen any of the others?" he asked after he took his seat then laid a cloth napkin over his white shorts. I shook my head. He frowned while stirring some Splenda into his coffee. "I bet they won't show. I wasn't sure if you jocks would be into a butterfly farm."

"I'm into it," I said then bit into a crispy slice of bacon. I'd worry about cholesterol later. When I was thirty. Today I was still twenty-nine and living high on the hog.

Great. Pork puns. Such a funny dad joke. Next you'll be wearing socks with your sandals.

Mason's smile was infectious. I grinned back. And there we sat smiling at each other over eggs and mango wedges.

"It'll be just us two then," he finally said, breaking the spell that had held us. I nodded and ate. Conversation was sparse.

Our driver, whom I was happy to see was Esmar, led us

to a Jeep with the Sheltered Sands logo on the doors. We waited for another ten minutes before Mason told him to go after sending texts to the Rebels still in bed. Not that they'd worry about us or anything. We were grown men after all. Two grown men. Not a man and a little boy. Men. God above why had it taken me this long to fucking absorb that fact?

As Esmar chattered on cheerfully I took a long look at Mason from the back. He was a man all right. Lean as a whipcord but utterly masculine. Gone was the gangly youth who followed me and Eli every damn place we went. He'd grown into a beautiful man with a sharp mind and a love of helping others find their dreams.

Maybe he can help you find your dreams too, Xander.

"Here we are, gents!" Esmar announced as we slowed to a stop. My gaze lingered on Mason for a second then moved to Esmar. He turned to smile at me. "I'll be back at noon if that's still good for the pick-up?"

"Yep, that's perfect," Mason said as he climbed off the Jeep.

"Perfect," I mumbled while futzing with my seatbelt.

"It sticks. Push and pull. There you go!" Esmar said then grinned. I somehow got out of the back without falling on my face and waved at the Jeep as it pulled off. Then I peeked to the side to see Mason slipping on a pair of sunglasses with bright orange frames. They matched the tangerine tank top he wore. The man was always so colorful. I liked that about him. I liked a great deal about him if I were being honest.

"We ready?" He looked up at me. People milled around us, adults and children and old people. I longed to kiss him just because he looked so perfectly Mason. And he made me happy, giddy, crazy.

Crazy enough to dream with?

"Yeah, ready," I replied. He bounced off. I trundled along behind him marveling at how he was easily the most beautiful sight on this island. Over the next few hours, he had some heavy competition with the stunning beauty surrounding us. We walked through a lush tropical forest with flowers of every shape, color, and scent all around us. And the butterflies. Holy hell, I had never seen so many of them. Various shades of blue, yellow, orange, black, and red. Most I had no clue about, but I did see several monarchs. They flitted about inside the huge enclosure. A big blue one landed on Mason's head. I used my phone to snap a picture. Then a swallowtail, or what I think was a swallowtail, took a rest on my shoulder. Mason circled me, snapping away, gabbling nonstop as he took image after image.

We lingered for a good hour inside the enclosure watching the delicate beauties fly from flower to flower. Mason stood so close that his arm was in constant contact with mine. I didn't mind. Once, when a blueish moth landed nearby, I pulled him close to snap a selfie of us and the moth on the netting. He gave me a startled look but settled nicely into my side. I held him there for a long time after I'd snapped the picture. He leaned into me after a bit, his head resting on my chest, his camera up at his face. Contentment flooded me. So, we stood there by the blue moth for a long time, my arm around his shoulder.

"We should go. Our ride will be here soon," he said then looked up to see if I'd heard him.

I had. And I was planning to say something but my whole being was wrapped up in his face, lost in his eyes, hungry for his lips.

"I want to kiss you," I whispered.

"Go ahead," he softly replied.

I lowered my mouth to his. It was tentative at first, flighty and soft like the winged wonders all around us. But the taste and feel of him soon loosened the unease. He flicked his tongue over my lower lip. I softly moaned before twisting around to face him and deepen the kiss. His hands skittered up my sides, making me gasp at the ticklish sensations. I slid my arms around him, pressing him close, and was about to rub my hard dick against his when a child nearby giggled. A woman behind us made a tsking sound. I released him, lifted my head, and stared at his heavy-lidded face. A face as familiar as my own but so much more beautiful. A face that held dreams and fantasies. Could they be mine? Did we dare?

"Do you believe in dreams?" I asked as my head swam with forbidden possibilities.

"Of course." He rose to his toes to brush a timid peck over my mouth. "Are you dreaming about something in particular?"

"Maybe." My head was filled with gossamer nonsense. Silly romantic fluff that would, I was sure, evaporate like fog when the sun touches it. "Your brother… "

"Will have to deal." He stepped back, took my hand, and led me from the enclosure. Gripping his thin fingers tightly like the lifeline they were, I plodded along beside him, unable to sort through the mishmash of warring thoughts. Esmar awaited us at the brightly painted welcome sign. He said nothing about us holding hands. Guess he was used to gay people. Few of the tourists had cared either. A couple might have looked askance but no one said anything.

We both rode in the back. Mason at my side, his fingers still woven with mine. The wind whistled around us, Mason's thick hair whipping about. I wanted to touch it so badly but just couldn't bring myself to do so in front of our driver. Maybe, someday, with someone to guide me, I'd be able to engage in PDAs like the rest of the world.

The ride back to the hotel went by quickly. Mason and I didn't talk much. He just remained nestled into my side, his thumb rubbing over my wrist, his smile wistful and filled with promise. I think I tipped Esmar before we bumbled into the hotel lobby and past the registration desk.

And then there we were. Staring at a long corridor of doors. Mason gave my hand a squeeze to pull me from the sight of his door.

"Nothing more has to happen today," he assured me.

"I want more to happen."

"Are you sure?"

"Yes. I am sure. I'm tired of living on the empty side of the glass."

He lifted my scarred knuckles to his pink lips—from now on pink was my favorite color—and led me slowly to his room. My heart was hammering in my chest as he scanned the key. The beep and click nearly made my knees buckle.

Somehow we managed to get inside and place his new camera on the desk before we pounced on each other. Mason was a wonderful kisser. His tongue was slick and talented. I lifted him from the floor, his tight ass cradled in my palms. With a grunt he wound around me like a jungle vine, legs around my waist, arms looped around my neck. Each swipe of his tongue over mine made me shudder. I wanted to weep in joy but opted to carry him to the bed instead. We fell into it, his hands sliding under my shirt as I nipped at his plump lower lip.

"Off," he huffed as I wedged a leg between his thighs. I sat back, ripped off my shirt and threw it across the room. He wiggled free of his tank top, and I was left gobsmacked by the svelte beauty of his body. I ran my fingertips over his chest, around his dark pink—I love pink!—nipples and marveled as they pebbled. He rolled and writhed under me, his prick stiff as a new pencil. "You okay?"

I nodded. "Just... I've never been here before. I don't know how to love you as I want to. Please don't let me hurt you. What if I hurt you. What if I'm just too rough—"

"You'll do fine. I'll show you." He reached for my cock, rubbing it through my pants. I gasped and bucked. He smiled at me as his fingers tugged down the zipper of my shorts. My cock was heavy and hot and eager. It pushed free of my briefs. Mason purred like a puma as his fingers wrapped around my length.

"God," I panted as I ripped at the button of his shorts, sending the silver circlet flying. "Sorry."

"Fuck don't be sorry. I love how hot you are for me."

I fell over him, capturing his mouth, licking deep. I ran my tongue over his teeth then sparred with him as I fished out his dick. He sucked in a sharp inhalation when I fisted his long, lean cock.

"Mm, fuck, yeah. Both of us. I want to feel your cock

next to mine," he growled, and I was happy to oblige. My hand barely fit around us both. He wiggled his fingers between us to cup my hand. "Xander, oh shit. Pump. Harder. Fuck yeah. Fuck yeah!"

Hearing my name burst out of him on such a passionate shout was all it took for me. I let the tingles in my spine overtake me as Mason covered our fingers with spunk. The hot rush of semen coated our cocks. I grunted and spewed all over our hands and stomachs. Mason grabbed my head, left hand over my right ear, and kissed me with hot, wet swipes of tongue.

"God, ah God," I huffed into his mouth as my hips twitched. He nibbled at my lips then along my jaw, his nails scraping my scalp, his ass leaving the bed as we milked ourselves and each other.

"So good. So, so good." He tasted me again as we struggled for each breath. I sat back, easing my weight off him. His eyes met mine and they were still smoldering. He lifted his sticky fingers to his mouth then slid them between his lips.

"Holy hell," I moaned at the sight. He cleaned his hand off then grabbed mine by the wrist. A tremor ran through me as he flicked his tongue between my fingers to get every warm droplet of our combined cum. "Never seen anything so hot."

He sucked on my thumb, which made my dick swell with surprising speed. Uncaring of the damage caused, we kicked off our shorts, ignoring the rip of a seam or the pop of a zipper. I had to be naked with him. Right now, or I might die. Mason moved over me and humped me until I was on the cusp then he wiggled down between my legs.

Eyes locked with mine; he took the fat purple head of my dick into his mouth. Starbursts exploded outward from my balls. I pumped a load down his throat. He swallowed it with noisy, greedy humming sounds. I was wrung out after the second mind-altering orgasm but had enough in me to flip him to his back, spread his toned thighs, and settle between them to suck him off. He came with a shout and lots of clawing. My shoulders burned from his nails, but I couldn't care less.

He whispered my name lovingly as he came. I'd never had that before. Hell, most of the men I hooked up with didn't know my name and there had been a reason for that. But now, with Mason, I could share what made me Xander with him. I could love him fully. I kissed my way up his slim body to his lips. They were dark pink and puffy. I touched mine to his. He gathered me close and kissed me with such devotion it made my eyes wet.

"I'll show you to your dreams," he whispered as he pulled the covers up over us then snuggled up tight.

"I love you, Mason."

He sighed softly against my hair, "And I love you."

"We're good then?"

"A long way past good, and on to awesome."

As I lay there with him tight to my side, I knew things would never be the same from this day on. Nor did I want them to be. Whatever came of this, of *us*, we'd face it down. It was that simple. I wasn't about to let this walking dream go.

Chapter Ten

Mason

THE ALARM WAS AN OBNOXIOUS BASTARD THING THAT needed to sort out its life. God knows why it had gone off, given it was five a.m., and I was on vacation. I reached for the phone, randomly pressing buttons until raucous music faded into nothing, and then stretched the kinks from my exhausted body before rolling back on my side to check on Xander. We had a ton of things we needed to talk about this morning, not least of which was how we were going to keep this a secret for now, and how we were going to keep our hands off each other. Also, it was his birthday, and I thought I could wake him up with a birthday blowjob if the alarm hadn't already spoiled that idea.

Only there was no sign of Xander, and the bed wasn't warm, the sheet pushed back and his side empty. My chest hollowed, and a rush of pain consumed me—he'd made a choice and given up on me. On us.

I had to live with that. Just because I loved him, it

didn't mean he had reciprocal feelings or even wanted to run the gamut of emotions and conversations that we'd have to deal with.

A cool breeze whispered into the room from the open door to the patio, and the voile there moved gently. I spotted a flash of color, immediately rolling off the mattress and shoving my feet into shorts and yanking them up, forgetting the button was gone so they slipped to my hips. I stumbled over discarded bedding and scrubbed my eyes as I headed for the door and out into the early morning. Xander was staring out at the ocean, cross-legged, hands resting on his knees and his back straight. He wore the shirt from last night, open and loose, and he'd pulled his shorts back on. He looked calm, from the back at least.

"Morning," he half-whispered. Given Eli was right next door maybe he was whispering to avoid being discovered outside my room. But then, why was he sitting right there in the open, and why make it so obvious? Shouldn't he be hiding away with me, so we could keep our big secret?

I stopped beside him and then dropped to sit next to him, our knees touching. "Happy birthday," I whispered back.

"Thank you."

"Do you feel any different?"

"Being thirty, no. But finally admitting I'm in love with my best friend's brother, yes."

Uh oh. "What are you doing out here?" *Where anyone can see you?*

"Thinking." He reached out for a hand, and I took his without hesitation. "About how we do this."

"Do what?"

He looked troubled, uncertain. "I thought you wanted us to be together?"

"I do, God, you don't know how much. I didn't mean about *us*. I meant about everything else."

"You mean the world, the press, Eli?" He smiled then and squeezed my hand. "I need to be honest with everyone, and I'm not sure how's Eli going to take it."

I scooted a little nearer, and he released my hand and gathered me close to him, hugging me briefly and then laying his arm over my shoulder as I leaned in.

"He'll forgive us in the end," I murmured, although we both knew that wasn't entirely true.

He sighed heavily then shook his head. I didn't want him to be thinking bad things right now. I wanted him to have the happiest thirtieth birthday ever.

"Do you remember your birthday?"

"Which one? I've had a few."

He shot me a look, and I saw the narrowing of his eyes. "When you turned eighteen."

I stiffened in Xander's hold because I knew where this was going. That was the single night where Eli had turned from being a loving older brother to a man convinced the entire world was out to hurt me. Aarni Lankinen had cornered me in the kitchen where I'd been sulking because I'd fought with Becca, stupid to look back on it, but I'd been young and stupid, and three beers was enough to make me an idiot. Abruptly, I needed Xander to hold me closer when I shivered with the memory of that night.

"You mean what happened at the party."

"I wanted to kill Aarni," Xander said. "I wanted to put my hands around his neck and squeeze the life out of him. I could have, you know, and it would have solved so much. Bryan Delaney, Henry Greenaway, Tennant Rowe, what Aarni did to those others, using his size and his anger to try to force you—"

"What stopped you?" I interrupted because I didn't want to think about the guilt I carried for what he'd done to the other men. Or remember the way Aarni had pushed me against the refrigerator, hard against me, grinding against me, telling me all kinds of horrible things. I'd just stood there, not knowing what to do, and it was only Becca coming into the kitchen that had stopped it from going any further. I was small compared to a twenty-one-year-old physical hockey player. I was *weak*. Becca had seen though, and it had to be her that told Eli.

"You stopped me."

"Me?"

"Do you remember what you said to Eli?"

"Not completely. I thought he was the one who wanted to kill Aarni, not you."

"Eli wanted to kill him for what he did to you, but I would have done anything to make sure you still had Eli in your life. If he'd hurt Aarni, then you might lose the only family you had. So there was me, holding Eli back, and you have to remember that Eli was white-hot with temper… "

"I never wanted Eli to know, or you. Or anyone." I sighed and leaned closer to Xander, tucking myself into his neck. "Even now I have a ton of regrets about that night. If

I'd gone to the authorities, if I'd said something, then what happened to Tennant, and the others, would never have happened. It was on me."

Xander shoved my shoulder just enough to let me know he didn't agree with that at all. I'd had enough counseling that I knew it wasn't my fault, but even now I couldn't quite look Brady Rowe in the eyes in case he ever found out that I'd done nothing.

"So, you were standing there, with bruises still on your arm, and Becca holding your hand, and Eli and I were in kill mode, and you just looked right at us and said that you'd already lost two people you loved, and you couldn't bear to lose anyone else."

"I remember," I admitted as the memories flooded back. Aarni had left the party, and Becca had sought out Eli, and where Eli was, Xander was, and I knew it wasn't going to end well.

Aarni *just* held me against my will.

Aarni *just* whispered what he wanted to do to me.

Aarni *just* said that he could show me what it was like to know what a real man could do.

None of that was enough to go to the police. At least that is what I'd told myself. All I could think about was that if I'd accused him of anything when I'd been drinking, only eighteen, and maybe it had been my fault? Then for the two men I loved fighting over who was going to kill Aarni first, right in front of me, I couldn't bear to think of losing either of them.

"We reported it, management eventually traded him to the Raptors, and now after what he did, he's serving jail time for being the bastard he is. But you still have us, and you will always have us."

We sat in silence for a while, and all the soft glow from last night, the connection and the love, was cold in the light of day.

"I'm too big, too clumsy off skates. I don't know my own strength, and I could hurt you."

I shook my head and pressed a kiss to his neck, feeling him shiver and press against my lips. "You could never hurt me."

"I wouldn't mean to—"

"Never."

"I will try every second to be the best man I can be for you."

He sighed then and tipped my chin to kiss me with the gentlest of touches, not deepening the connection but pressing the promise into my skin. Then we were quiet again and time seemed to pass molasses slow as the sun climbed from dawn and into full day. People began to walk on the beach, and still we didn't move. Dunny ambled along the shoreline just after seven, staring out to the horizon, not looking our way lost in his thoughts. It was close enough that we had to decide what came next.

"Last night I said I didn't know how to love you as I want to."

I chuckled and kissed him again with a leer. "I'll show you." Only he captured my face in his hands and cradled me there, staring at me with emotion bright in his eyes.

"I didn't mean that. Well, it's partly that, but it's not *just* the sex side. It's Eli. It's family. It's your new business and changes in the team. It's not knowing what to do for the best but absolutely sure about what comes first."

"Eli."

He released his hold on me, and I moved with my back to the ocean, facing him, our knees touching. "I want to be completely honest with Eli, like properly old-fashioned. Ask him if it's okay, explain to him that I won't hurt you and that I'll love you the best I can for as long as I can. Maybe I could talk about kids, or my 401k, or the fact that Brady wants to put my name forward for captain if he leaves." He bit his lip then. "Pretend I didn't say that last bit."

I mimicked a zip on my lips. "I want to tell Eli as well. I want to tell him I love you, that I've loved you since I knew what love was, and I want to love you the best I can for as long as I can as well. Maybe I'll mention kids and my pathetically small 401k, and I promise not to mention the captain thing." I leaned forward and added softly, "But that is so cool."

He smiled at me, a small hint of pride in his expression. "Not sure if it will happen, I mean, we're getting heat for me being… yeah, you know."

"Everyone knows you're the bravery and heart of the team."

He wrinkled his nose and then got serious. "So we agree then. We're telling Eli, up front and honest, and if he hates it then we… do what?"

"That's simple," I said with a smile that didn't reflect the worry in my thoughts. "We move to Aruba on a permanent basis. I'll take up a bartender job, and you can teach hockey."

He raised a single eyebrow. "Not sure there would be many takers for hockey in Aruba."

"So we'll live off my tips." I lowered my voice. "And your *enormous* 401k."

He snorted a laugh and it felt lighter, but I knew we were both consumed with the worry of what we wanted to do. Eli was so protective of me. His way of dealing with losing Mom and Dad was to pour everything into his career and to me. He'd made it to the top in hockey, and he had the best little brother in the entire world if I say so myself, but how would he feel if the two people closest to him were hooking up? Would he feel like the odd one out? It could be so good, to extend the family, and maybe he'd give in and finally date someone for longer than a week. Then there would be four of us, and I knew I'd love whoever caught Eli, and then there would be kids, and we'd be this huge rambling family.

"We should tell him."

Xander nodded, and we stood and hugged each other briefly before separating and grinning at each other like idiots. Somehow, whatever we had to do today, everything was going to be okay.

"He'll probably be asleep still," Xander said.

"Then we'll break into his room and sit on him until he wakes up. Whatever, we have to tell Eli before we do anything else."

"Tell Eli what?"

I turned slowly. Eli was there, with a wrapped gift in his arms, decorated with a gaudy silver bow. We'd chosen the gift together, a memory book filled with pictures of Eli and Xander, me and Eli, me and Xander, all three of us, and the plan had been to meet early and give it to him.

Hence the alarm. I set that when I'd wanted to shower, shave, and look as hot as I could to surprise Xander, that was before we'd ended up in bed and everything had changed. *Shit.*

Eli was grinning, probably psyched to see the two of us already standing there and ready to hand over the gift, but slowly the grin paled, and instead his chin took on a stubborn tilt.

"What do you need to tell me? What the fuck is going on?"

Chapter Eleven

Xander

SOMETIMES NO MATTER HOW YOU'VE PREPPED FOR something it was never going to be easy.

Keeping my mind from diving into the gutter I gave Mason a small smile then turned to face his brother. My best friend. This was going to suck. Still, it had to be done. I'd spent too many years hiding things from the world. I was not going to sneak around with Mason. That would make what we felt for each other cheap and dirty. To me it was neither of those things. It was glorious. Rapturous. Enlightening. Man, I was tossing around a lot of religious terms for a man who didn't do religion. Maybe if spending time in church felt like holding Mason in my arms I might just start attending.

Eli stepped closer to place my gift on the small glass table. "Okay, what the fuck has happened? You two look like you robbed a bank? Oh hell, are you going all *Point Break* on me?"

We tried to laugh at the comment. That had been a huge movie for us when we were younger. Eli always wanted to be Patrick Swayze and I longed to be Keanu. Poor Mason was just one of the grubby underlings in a dead president's mask. The things we made him do. It was a wonder he could even stand me let alone love me. *He loved me.*

"Seriously, someone needs to get talking. Did Dunny streak along the beach again?" Eli prompted.

"No, nothing like that," I hurried to say. No, thank God. One streaking Dunny incident had been enough to last me for ages. "It's nothing bad. Sit down."

He eyeballed us both then dropped into a chair, the metal legs grinding across the cement. Mason took his seat between us. I had to assume he thought he would leap up and break up any fisticuffs that would break out. As we both had several inches and probably forty pounds on him playing ref was cute. Unrealistic but cute. Although Eli would never take a swing with Mason in the vicinity. He loved his brother too much and knew his own strength. Maybe having him there was a good idea after all. I did *not* want a bloody nose on my birthday. I'd heard the stories from Brady about his reaction to hearing Jared and his baby brother had been lovers. It hadn't been pretty.

"Is someone sick?" Eli asked, his shoulders drawn up around his ears, tension deepening the furrows of his brow.

"No, it's nothing bad," I reiterated. I wished we had food out here or something to drink. Anything to give me something to do with my hands. At the moment, they were tapping madly on my thighs. Then, as if to say "Enough!" Mason reached over to take my right hand. He slid his fingers between mine and threw his jaw up as he did when he was feeling spunky.

"Xander and I are going to start dating," he announced as if he were telling his brother about the weather. My gaze flew from Mason to Eli. I'd been hoping to build up to the announcement. Ease him into it by pointing out all my good qualities.

Eli sniggered. We sat there hands clasped. Eli snorted. We sat there. Eli wet his lips as the bemused smile he was wearing disappeared.

"Are you… " He scratched his nose, a sure sign he was confused. "You're serious?"

My fingers tightened around Mason's. Suddenly, I was struck speechless. Some great captain I'd make. Freezing up when the shit hit the fan.

"Yes," I coughed out. Mason nodded. Eli gawked and scratched his nose again.

"Since when?" Eli asked after a full moment of utter, deadly silence had fallen over us.

"I've loved Xander forever," Mason said, his gaze touching mine. I felt like the gift on the table. Wrapped up and ready for the right person to unwrap me. To remove the lid that had kept me in the dark for so long. To expose me to the light and warmth. Mason was pulling the ribbons free that had bound me for so many years. "It was just recently that we got over ourselves and admitted how we felt."

"You did that for me," I said, my voice so gruff that it sounded like someone else speaking. Mason smiled softly. The urge to pull him into my lap and hold him forever was strong. "You took off my lid." Mason's brows beetled in confusion. "That sounded much better in my head."

"Whoa. Just… fucking *whoa*," Eli coughed out. I tore my gaze from Mason to stare at my oldest and dearest friend. "Just… fucking whoa." He scrubbed at his face with his hands so hard I worried he might melt his face with sheer friction. "Okay. This is… " His hands fell to his lap. He looked at me then his brother. "You've loved him forever?"

"Yep," Mason replied, popping the P then giving me a loving glance that made my toes curl. God this man did things to me with a single look that I'd never dared to imagine I would experience. "For ages." His attention went back to Eli whose face was slack. Which was better than furious.

"Ages," Eli mumbled. His gaze flickered to me. "Do not tell me that you've been eyeballing my little brother for ages. Because, dude, I will clean your fucking clock."

"No, not for ages. Definitely not ages. But for a long time now I've had feelings for him that were way beyond friendship. But I wasn't out, and he was off-limits."

"Yes, okay!" Eli sat up and pointed at me. "Yes, off-limits. See, that's the word my fucked brain was searching for."

"It's two words," Mason commented.

"Do not grammar me right now!" Eli snapped before closing his eyes to do some yogic breathing. "I will not yell. I will not yell. I will not yell."

Mason smiled at me, and I sensed that things might be okay. Hopefully.

"Okay, so off-limits. Why is he now on-limits? Mason,

I swear if you tell me that's not a real word, I will feed your measly ass to the damn seagulls." I looked skyward. There were quite a few gulls gliding overhead now. Seeking out the warm currents so they could climb into the new day. That was me. I was a gull. Just call me Xander Livingston Seagull. God, I really needed to stop borrowing books from my parents.

"He's on-limits now because I let down my walls and let him in," I replied with candor.

Eli studied me intently, his lips flat to his teeth, his finger rubbing the side of his nose. "Uh-huh. Walls. Right. I'm not… I need to let this sink in. I'm trying hard not to punch you in the face for wheeling my little brother."

"It's appreciated," I said, Mason's fingers pinched between mine.

"Can we get something to eat and drink here? Something with vodka? What are those drinks you like when you drag me to Bella Mare for brunch, Skid?"

Mason made such a face that I had to snigger. Skid. Man. I'd not heard that nickname for him for probably twenty years. Poor Mason. You have one potty accident when you're five. Of course, their mother had nixed that name as soon as she'd heard it, saving Mason from the taunting that only an older brother could deliver. I still missed their parents. They'd been good people.

"I hate you," Mason grumbled but shook free of my death grip to ring up for some breakfast from the main desk. "We'd like three continental breakfasts and three mimosas sent to room eight while the bill is to go to room ten, right on my brother's credit card because he's being a jerk."

Eli ignored Mason, his attention lingering on me. "You need to promise me that you will never hurt him," he stated forcefully. "I love you, man. You're like my twin, Xan. If you hurt my brother, I will be forced to beat the shit out of you. That would break my heart. So just don't hurt him. Ever. He's all I have in this world. My family. It's all right here at this table and I do *not* want to lose either of you. So, I'm going to be cool. I'm going to have a mimosa or twelve when they get here, and I'm going to say I wish you well. But keep in mind that I will bust you up if you make him cry. And I mean like bad crying not the crying he does when he stubs his toe or watches some goofy chick flick."

"The fact that you *don't* cry when watching *Steel Magnolias* proves that you have no soul," Mason parried as he reached out to take Eli's big, scarred hand. A hand that looked much like mine.

I did the same. I stretched over the table to offer Eli my hand. Mason grabbed my other and there we sat, three men holding hands.

"All we need to do is break into a chorus of 'Kumbaya,'" Eli snarked, breaking the tender moment. Which was fine, and totally Eli. He wasn't one for big emotional displays. Truth be told, I wasn't either but today was such a momentous day that a little emo was fine.

"Thanks, man." I gave Eli's thick fingers a squeeze then lifted Mason's smaller hand to my lips. I kissed his knuckles, my eyes only for him now. "I promise I will never make you ugly cry."

"Will you make me weep with sexual pleasure?" Mason asked breathlessly just like a 50s movie starlet.

"And *that's* as much as I can hear this early in the morning. Where the fuck are those mimosas?" Eli barked as he shoved to his feet to walk off his unease. Mason winked at me. I could do nothing but grin like a man who'd just found the winning lottery ticket tucked away in his wallet.

———————

BY THE TIME MIDNIGHT CAME I TRULY DID FEEL LIKE Charlie Bucket.

Only my golden ticket didn't take me to a chocolate factory, it carried me to Mason's arms. I'd hardly drank all day long, instead content to stuff copious amounts of food into my face while watching my buddies get shitfaced. Also, there was the added caveat that Mason was at my side, tucked in close, throughout the day. Renco, Marquis, and Dunny were thrilled for us. Eli… well, he was taking a bit longer to come to terms with us kissing on the sly. He'd finally made it a drinking game, announcing to our group that every time we locked lips shots had to be downed. Which explained why they were all drunken sots that we'd poured into their beds one by one.

"So on a scale from one to ten how do you rate your thirtieth birthday?" Mason enquired after we hoisted Dunny into his bed. Given he was naked we didn't have to undress him as we had the previous three.

I pulled him close. "It would be far better if I hadn't had to witness Dunny's dick flopping in the wind as he danced the Tumba on the tabletop."

"Yeah. He's pretty light on his feet considering his size

and the amount of booze he ingested." Mason kissed me on the chin then led me from Dunny's room. I followed along, shopping bags filled with gifts in one hand, his fingers meshed with mine. "Your place or mine?" he asked as we slowly made our way down the hall.

"We don't have to do anything tonight if you don't want."

He gave me a wicked look then tugged me to his door. I stumbled behind, my feet feeling incredibly big and flappy right now. We were inside his room in a heartbeat, my bag filled with memories, candy, booze, ten boxes of condoms, and a gallon jug of lube courtesy of Dunny taken from my fingers and placed on the desk.

"Trust me, I want. You'll need the condoms and lube," Mason announced as he sashayed to the wide bed, shedding clothing as easily as a cat sheds fur. My gaze touched on his spine, the sway of his lean hips, and the curve of his buttocks. He flung himself on top of the bed, rolled to his back, and let his lean legs flop open. My dick was pushing against the zipper of my shorts, eager for the bounty that was now spread out before me. Mason took himself in his hand and began stroking his hard dick. "Do you like to top or bottom?"

"I've… I'm versatile. Yeah, I'm pretty sure that would be good. Either way."

His fingers stalled. "Have you never fucked before?"

"No, no anal. That was a rule. Sex yeah but blowjobs only." I felt like a fool. A man of thirty years who had never once been fucked.

"Well, seeing as how you were only hooking up with strangers when you could sneak it in that's a damn smart rule. I'm negative and take PrEP and always used condoms so you can feel safe in case of breakage or some mishap."

"I'm not scared of catching anything from you," I tossed out unthinking of what was tumbling from my piehole.

"You can catch things from anyone. Never forget that. Well, you won't have to worry though." He resumed petting his cock. "I don't share."

"Me either."

"Good. Then come here and let me show you a few things." He tugged on his nuts. My dick throbbed in time with my pulse. I shucked off my clothes with haste. "Damn you have a fat dick. Bring it here. I want to suck on it." Hands filled with condoms and a jug of lube under my arm, I hurried to join him on the bed. I flung the goodies to the mattress then laid down over him, my mouth sealing over his. His cock lay beside mine, hard and hot, and his fingers... God but his fingers were light little tickles of delight that skipped and danced over my skin. As we sucked on each other's mouths, he found my ass, his fingertips sliding between my cheeks. I gasped into his mouth when he found my hole.

"Yes, more," I grunted then rolled to my back, taking him with me.

"You like that?" He settled between my thighs, his eyes simmering, his lips swollen from our rough kisses. "You want me to get into you? Work you open with my fingers and tongue then fuck you?"

"Shit... shit... " His words were so dirty, so hot. "Yes, do that. Please." I grabbed my knees and eagerly pulled my thighs to my chest. I'd watched porn. I knew the mechanics quite well. What I didn't know was how incredible it actually felt to have a man bury his face in your ass. I shuddered and whimpered as Mason tongued my ass. The room was thick with the sounds of his mouth on my hole combined with my groans of ecstasy. He worked me open slowly, his tongue leading the way for his fingers. I gasped and clawed when he found my prostate. His lips stretched over my cock as he fingered me into delirium.

"Close… Mason… " I panted as he added a third finger while his tongue dipped into the slit of my dick. His gaze was molten. My balls tightened up when his eyes met mine. Fuck he looked good with my cock in his mouth. "Want to come… you in me. Please."

He popped off, his chin and lips slick with spittle, and suited up as our gazes held. "You sure you want to bottom?"

Oh, I was sure. I wanted to feel him in me. "Yes, fuck me."

"Shit," he growled, pumping lube all over his hand, my thigh, and the bed. Who cared? I gave no fucks right now. I'd sleep in a vat of lube and semen if he would just hurry. "You need to relax. Breathe. It'll burn for a bit but then, baby, it'll rock your world."

"Hurry," I gasped, my cock leaking all over my belly. He knelt right by my ass, his cock resting on my hole, then he hooked my heels over his shoulders. I grasped at his thighs, the tug of hair making him wince but not slowing his entry. "Breathe. Come on, Xan, relax. Let me in."

I closed my eyes and exhaled. The fat head of his prick pressed in. The burn was intense, but I'd suffered much worse on the ice. Not in my ass obviously but a little burn would not bench me. No fucking way. Then he was easing in, deeper, deeper, stealing my breath that he kept telling me to use. How could I? I was filled with Mason. There was no room for oxygen.

"You okay?" he asked, his voice strained. I opened my eyes, licked at the sweat on my upper lip, and found him watching me with concern. "You look tight. I mean… not that way tight because fucking hell I *know* you're tight down here. Tight mentally."

"I just… need a second. You've got a huge dick."

He grinned. "Thanks, but not really. Not like yours." He bent down, bending me into a pretzel, to steal a kiss. I moaned at the change of sensation. He flicked his hips. A cry of pleasure broke free from deep within me. "Yeah, there you go. Relax and feel me inside you."

"I feel you," I whispered then gave myself over to the slick thrusting motion that was now the center of my universe. The ache and stretch eased away a little, the rub of his cock against that bundle of nerves soon had me spurting all over myself and my hand.

"*Fuck!*" Mason snarled as I blew apart. He tumbled over with me, his head snapping back and his cry of release a guttural sound that pulled another spurt of cum from me. I could feel his cock kicking inside me, the hot rush of semen as he filled the condom. It was everything. Beyond everything. It was Mason, and he was me, just as I was him. I reached up, my fingers gliding over his shoulder to his neck, biting into the nape, and I pulled his mouth down to mine.

Mason deflated slowly, my legs slipping off his

shoulders and his body puddling atop mine. I held him close, peppering his face and neck with tiny kisses. He sighed then sniggered when I blew into his ear. I led his mouth back to mine with a gentle touch of fingers to jaw.

"That was… incredible." He sighed between kisses. "I have to take care of this."

I let him move then, reluctantly releasing him. He eased out of me with care, removed the condom, tied it tight, then padded into the bathroom. I slowly sat up.

"Ouch, yeah, big dick," I muttered at the pull deep inside. Easing upward I joined him at the sink where he was brushing his teeth. I washed my belly and hands off then slid my arms around his middle, burying my nose in his tousled hair. "My ass hurts."

"I warned you," he said then spit and rinsed the sink. I held him close.

"No regrets whatsoever." I peeked around his head to find his gaze in the mirror. His eyes were lazy-lidded. He looked like a man well-loved, kind of how I appeared. Rumpled yes, but so sated. "Can I stay the night?"

"Of course." He wiggled around in my arms, his fingers carding through my damp hair. "It's your turn to top next." Oh damn. My flaccid dick thought that was a great idea. In half an hour or so. I *was* thirty now. I did need a little time to recharge. "Happy birthday to you."

"Happy birthday to me." I claimed his mouth in another kiss. I wished I could turn thirty every year just so I could relive this moment with this man over and over.

Chapter Twelve

Mason

"Can I ask you a question?"

I wasn't sure I was capable of talking, let alone answering questions this early in the morning. Not only had Xander just done one hell of a good job of topping, but he'd also made me wait until the point I was begging, and now wrung out we were flat on our backs on the bed staring up at the ceiling fan, fingers linked, and I for one was grinning like an idiot.

"Forty-two," I murmured.

"Huh?" We turned our heads to face each other. I loved how adorably confused he looked. In fact, I loved everything about him from his smile to his eyes to his belly, and his pecs, and his ass, and his deliciously gorgeous cock. Plus, his hockey playing skills and how sexy he looked on the ice was just one more facet to super-stud-Xan who clearly didn't get the pop culture reference.

"Forty-two is the answer to the Ultimate Question of

Life, the Universe, and Everything." I quoted from memory, which is kind of sad really when sometimes I'd forget which day it was yet could recall an obscure poster in one of my friend's dorm rooms. I turned on my side to face him fully and lost myself in his incredible eyes. "You don't look a day over twenty-nine," I whispered.

"Thank you, I think, but I still don't get forty-two, is that a math equation or something?" He frowned now, and I felt a tug of guilt. As the annoying bratty kid brother, I'd always teased Eli, and by extension Xander, about his lack of college smarts but it was only in retaliation for them messing with me over being a book nerd. I admired that Eli and Xander had an instinctive understanding of the sports world they inhabited that I didn't have. Hell, I've never met two more quick to calculate the path of a puck or understand the different ways that each one of a hundred skaters could come at them.

"It's a quote from a book, sorry, you were going to ask a question?"

"But what is forty-two?"

I kissed the question away because he was all serious, and I wanted to pull him back to *his* subject, whatever it was. "What did you want to ask me."

I slid a little closer and kissed the end of his nose before leaning back.

"Something you said about loving me forever." He dipped his gaze shyly, and God, I wanted to gather him into my arms and never let him go.

"I wasn't lying. It feels like forever to me."

"You never said anything," he said. "Not that you could have, or could know that I was… that I would… "

I put him out of his misery. "You were like my big brother, only you were the one who didn't noogie me at every opportunity or steal my scale model of the Millennium Falcon just to see if it could actually fly from the attic window."

"Well, I might have mentioned that I wanted to see it fly," Xander admitted and winced.

"Was it you who then took it up three flights of stairs to throw it off the roof?"

"Well, no, but—"

"It wouldn't have mattered if you did because of course I loved you. Adored you."

"Yeah, but what about the day you thought you loved me? How did you know? I didn't tell anyone I was into guys, so didn't you feel sad?"

He was worried about me, and that was just another reason why I loved him.

"It started as hero worship, that was the start, but I can easily remember the day it became a proper love. You sure you want to hear this?"

"Did I do something impossibly sexy without realizing it?" He wiggled his eyebrows, and I shoved him.

"No. Well yes, you probably did, but I was newly out, and I had the hots for you big time. You and that guy from the ad for the cologne that... anyway, I digress. Hero worship turned to obsession the year of the Eric Staal birthday when you turned eighteen. Remember?"

Our two families, neighbors since before Eli and Xander had been born, made a big thing of birthdays, but this particular year had been special. Turning a fancy old age like eighteen meant a backyard barbecue, deck hockey, and so many presents for the boy next door that I thought the table might break. I'd saved money from a paper delivery route to buy him a hockey card. It wasn't the most expensive card. I couldn't get him a rare Mario Lemieux trader or find a single mention of a Wayne Gretzky card anywhere in my measly twenty-three dollar budget, but I did manage to get him a special edition Eric Staal which I knew he was missing from his collection.

I wanted to give him something to remember me by. Something that proved I wasn't the idiot kid my brother called me.

"Yeah, I remember." He smiled softly then.

"You and Eli were leaving Minnesota and heading to the Rebels training camp and walking right out of my life, which sounds dramatic when I look back on it. After all, I would be going to see games with Mom and Dad, and you'd be coming home when you could, still, it was all wrong. I just felt like my world was shifting, and at fourteen, knowing I was different, struggling with my feelings and my own life, I didn't want things to change."

"It must have been hard to be left behind. I'm sorry," Xander murmured.

"It was okay. I had friends at school. I still had Mom and Dad then, but you had hockey, and you and Eli had all the luck. Not only did you end up going to training camp at the same freaking NHL team, but Eli had some money to buy you a really cool gift."

"The stick. I still have that you know, it's battered and broken, but it's at the back of my coat closet."

"You were really happy about the stick, and all I had was a stupid little trading card, but even though it was tiny, you were just as excited to get that from me. You went and got your folder and made this huge fuss about finding the right sleeve to slip it into."

"I loved that card. Eric was the only Staal missing from my collection. It was the perfect present." He pressed kisses to my face and whispered against each eyelid that he loved me.

"If you keep doing that I won't be able to finish my story." I pushed him away, just a little. "Anyway, you side hugged me, told me it was perfect, and said you'd miss me when you moved away for good, and that was the moment I fell in love. I knew it wouldn't come to anything because you know"—I waved at him—"being straight and all that. But any man I've ever been with had to measure up to you and the fantasies I had about what it would be like to be with you for real."

He growled low in his chest, rolled over on top of me, and pinned me to the bed. "You're mine now," he said with a show of possession, grinning then kissing me all over. He rocked against me until I was impossibly hard and needy then slid down my body to kiss my thighs, followed by my belly, and woke me up properly with the best blowjob of my life.

Of course it was only polite to return the favor, and we giggled when I nearly fell off the bed, laughed when the shower wouldn't warm up, sighed when we kissed under the water, and then finally we were dressed and leaving the privacy of the room.

We had breakfast to ourselves, no sign of any of the other Rebels, but I didn't imagine they would surface for the rest of the day. There was a reason I'd thought I'd be spending a day of chilling after the birthday, imagining it would be just me who was left standing. Never in my wildest dreams did I expect Xander to be sitting here with me. I thought he'd be just as dead to the world as Eli and had planned my own day of museum visits and walking. We'd chosen a table with a view of the ocean and ate bowls of fresh fruit, toast with jelly, and drank a ton of coffee. We didn't talk much at first, exchanging soft secretive smiles and utterly happy to be in each other's company.

"What's on our agenda today?" Xander sat back in his chair, patting his belly and tipping his face to the sun, and I stared. I could never in a million lifetimes get tired of looking at Xander.

"Actually, I didn't have anything planned because I thought you and Eli would be hungover, and the rest of the guys weren't even meant to be here."

He sent me a confused glance. "Huh?"

"It was supposed to be Eli and me surprising you, not the other guys as well, that was Eli's last minute idea, and why I've had to rearrange a load of things to add them on."

"Typical Eli. Gotta love that guy."

I tipped my head to the sun as well, and we sat back in our chairs hand in hand with our eyes closed. I could stay right here forever. Back home there were legalities to work through on the new partnership with Becca, our offices to fit out, and advertising budgets, and loans, and the fear of starting my life all over again. Never mind what kind of relationship Xander and I could have in public. It's one thing announcing you're bi, but it's something else when you have a real life partner. Would the press leave him alone? Would there be more slurs every time the Rebels lost? Would he actually get to be captain? Was that a step too far for any high-level team? As far as I was aware, no team captain had come out, and they already carried the burden of expectation without adding drama from the fans, management, and the press. My mood dipped. I couldn't imagine a life where I couldn't hold Xan's hands, or be in love with him the way I wanted, but I'd work around anything as long as he didn't tell me to go.

"That was a big sigh," he murmured.

"I sighed?"

"As if you carried the weight of the world on your shoulders."

I'd been the one pushing Xander, but the closer we got to going home the more the worry of what might happen poked at me.

"It won't be easy back home, what with everything. I mean, my new partnership with Becca and setting up the company, and the Boston fans and management, and what they'll make of you dating Eli's little brother."

"I can see the banners now, *keep it in the family*, or some shit," Xander laughed.

"I want you to be safe. So, we need to think about it—"

"Shhh," he interrupted my weird but insistent spiral and tightened his grip on my hand for a moment. "I can't speak for the Rebels fans, management, or team, or even for your new company, but for us, it's going to be easy." He sat up in his chair and tugged me closer. "We'll find our way through whatever life throws at us, together, because I love you."

"I love you too." The words were beautiful, and a

feeling of pure happiness filled my heart until I thought it would burst.

We grabbed water bottles before heading down to the ocean to walk off the big breakfast, following the shoreline with the wash of the waves cool on our feet and our fingers tightly laced. I had so many important questions I wanted to ask Xander, all those things I thought about in the best of my fantasies where we were together, but everything felt so delicate right now, and it hadn't been tested in the court of real life.

Stop catastrophizing, stay in the moment.

He stopped walking and pulled out his cell phone, releasing my hand and taking photos, all of which seemed to include me in one way or another, and then we took a ton of selfies with my phone as well.

"Just to remember the perfect first day of being together," he said when he pocketed his phone, and I jumped him for that, kissing him as he caught me and held me steady. We couldn't do anything but kiss because this was somewhere anyone could walk by, but he was right. Everything was perfect. Our love was new, and today was the very first day of the rest of our lives. There was no reason to believe that it wouldn't last.

We came to a rocky outcrop and climbed to the top, awkward and difficult in bare feet, but when we got halfway up, we found a place to sit. In the shade of a palm tree, with a cooling stream that ran down the rocks to the sea, I'd have been happy to stay here all day.

"We should hit some museums later," Xander said and relaxed back against the rocks.

"Are you sure? We don't have to."

"I like history."

"You do?" How did I not know this?

"Hockey history at least." He chuckled. "But I need my horizons broadened and who better to show me."

History was so in my wheelhouse. "Did you know that when Aruba was claimed by the Spanish it was a center for smuggling and piracy? Can you imagine calling this island your home to bury all your treasure?"

"That's the kind of history I like. We should probably buy a spade and try digging some holes, find the treasure, and then never leave the island."

"I think the team might miss you."

"Yeah, but if we hid here, they'd soon forget me."

"The mystery of the missing hockey player," I mused.

"The mystery of the missing hockey player and his sexy boyfriend," he corrected, and I felt a thrill run through me at the word boyfriend. It sounded possessive and hot and utterly perfect. I could be the very best boyfriend for him, and we'd be together forever.

"They'd make documentaries about you and show blurry photos of you in your pirate hat."

"And you'd be right beside me and believe me I'd make that hat look good." He flexed his arm, and I was getting hard just at the teasing tone in his voice and the fact he looked like a freaking sun god lying next to me. He trailed his free hand over my arm, and I don't know when he'd moved to face me, but there he was, a few inches from me, looking just about as beautiful as he ever did. I kissed him then, and his lips tasted of the ocean and sunshine and all the good things in life.

Now, *this* was the moment I could stay in forever.

Chapter Thirteen

Xander

I HATED TO SAY GOODBYE TO ARUBA BECAUSE IT WAS THE place where I'd fully come into myself. It was also where Mason and I had finally come together. It'd always hold a special place in my heart, but I was ready for the next phase of my life.

It struck me while taking our seats in first class that, once we jetted away from this island paradise, reality would be waiting. And while that reality could be— probably would be—bumpy, I was looking forward to it. Perhaps more than the others judging by the washed-out looks of my friends. No one seemed to be excited to get back to the real world other than me. Even Mason seemed reserved this morning. He'd been on the phone all morning as we'd packed. He was still on the phone as we boarded. I tried not to be hurt by his undivided attention to his new business. It would take a lot of his time, I knew that. Still, I'd been hoping for a last kiss under a palm tree or perhaps one last lazy morning in bed. But that hadn't happened. Guess reality had found us.

I sat across the aisle from Mason, who had wanted a window seat. Marquis was on my right looking dapper but drained. Eli was seated in front of his brother and Renco and Dunny were ahead of me. Renco had been tightly wound this morning, pulling on a ballcap and dark glasses as if he were trying to avoid the paparazzi or the feds. Goalies. Who knew what oddness bubbled away in their heads?

"Are you looking forward to getting home?" I asked Marquis. He made a small noise like a snort, only not because Marquis was way too elegant and classy to pig snort.

"The rest of my summer is packed with travel." He sighed as if seeing the world was something terrible.

"First world problems," I mumbled and got a dry look from the man in the Bruno Margo acid-washed jeans and plum polo shirt that I'd guess had set him back a cool two grand.

"I suppose." He sighed as he removed his sunglasses. "I enjoy traveling, I do, but my family has set up things for me. Destinations I couldn't care less about but my father's ill, and my uncle refuses to fly so someone has to represent the family business overseas."

"And that's you?" He nodded while twirling his shades back and forth. "What's your family business?"

"Plumbing."

Oh. That wasn't at all what I'd expected. "Do plumbers have overseas deals?"

"They do when they're Miller & Miller Plumbing. I'm

sure you've heard of them." I shook my head. His dark brown eyes flared. "Oh, well if you've ever strolled through Manhattan, London, Dubai, Tokyo, Mexico City, or Mumbai and looked at the skyscrapers while wondering who does the plumbing for over ninety percent of those huge buildings the answer is Miller & Miller Plumbing. My father and uncle own it and are looking to branch out more into Europe. And since my cousins are useless, it falls to me to fly all around the world to break bread with piddly little countries and charm the local governments."

"Life is rough," I tossed out. That made him smile a little. "Eating caviar with kings, prime ministers, presidents, and sheiks."

"Well, when you put it like that… " He chuckled. "I know I'm being bratty. I just had plans for the summer. I wanted to disengage from the family business and coach a tee-ball league for underprivileged Boston youth. Now I'm stuck on the family Lear flying from one boring ass dinner to another, talking about toilets. Most of the other guys are already gone. I hate to let the kids down, but I can't tell my family no either."

"I can take your tee-ball league if you want. I've literally nothing going on. I was going to go home but now that Mason and I are… you know, a couple, I want to stay in Boston with him."

His sour gaze dissipated. "Really? That would be amazing. Thank you. I'll text you the info and let them know you'll be coaching in my place. You'll love it. The kids are four to six so just the perfect age to get into sports."

"Cool." We fist bumped. I turned to smile at Mason,

but he was jabbering away to Becca. I'd tell him later about the tee-ball league. We had all the time in the world now. Settling back into my seat I felt a serenity settle over me that I'd not felt in… well, ever. My life was finally starting to look as if it was falling into place one incredible bit at a time. Maybe I should thank that asshole who'd tried to lean on me for cash. Without his push, I'd probably still be in the closet all alone. So yeah, thank you asshole.

I WASN'T THE LEAST BIT SURPRISED WHEN OUR CHEERY pilot announced that we'd be landing at Logan with some delay. Like seriously, what the hell else was new? As we circled, I kept shooting glances at Mason, who sat stiffly in his seat, phone in hand, eyes glued to the wing.

"See a monster out there?" I asked. His sleepy gaze moved to me.

"What?"

"On the wing. A monster." He stared at me as if I'd asked him if he'd seen a hippo in a tutu dancing *Swan Lake* back in economy. "Don't tell me you don't remember."

"Guess not?" He shrugged then scrubbed at his eyes.

"How could you forget? Eli and I used to watch those old *Twilight Zone* shows every Saturday night. There was one with William Shatner, and he's recovering from a nervous breakdown and sees this monster on the wing of the plane he's flying in. You really don't remember that?"

"No, sorry." He did put his phone down to focus on me. Which was nice. The rest of the guys were sleeping or watching movies. Earbuds in meant "do not disturb" to me, so I'd spent the flight thinking. Probably not a good thing but I was too wound up in this exuberant new love affair, and what our futures held, to nod off.

"I'm shocked that you don't recall it. It freaked you the hell out," I said then chuckled at the memory of a maybe five-year-old Mason losing his shit over that episode.

"Okay, so was I just mildly freaked out or totally Spooky Space Kook freaked out? I have levels of freaked out," he explained as a smile danced on his lips. Lips that needed kissing. And soon.

"What the hell is a Spooky Space Kook?"

"Dude, honestly? From *Scooby-Doo*?" I shrugged. "Do not tell me you don't remember *Scooby-Doo*. If you do, I am telling the Rebels you need a brain scan to check for concussion damage."

"Of course I remember *Scooby-Doo* but not that kooky space guy."

He tsked me soundly. "I'm not sure we can be a couple anymore." That made me snicker. "He was this big guy in a cheesy spacesuit with a skull in the headpiece. Made this creepy wailing laughing sound. That bastardly thing scared me to death. Every time it'd laugh, I'd cry."

"Oh yeah! I remember now. Eli and I would chase after you making that stupid sound until you cried and ran to your mother." He tapped his nose. "God, we were such assholes to you."

"The biggest assholes," he agreed far too readily.

I leaned over into the aisle so we could speak more quietly. "If you ever get scared at night, I'll hold you close until the scary things go away."

He smiled that soft, dopey lovestruck smile I'd seen in the mornings in Aruba.

"What happens when I'm home alone in that creepy pool house?" he teased. Eli's pool house was far from creepy. It was damn swanky.

"That's a problem. You'll just have to move in with me then," I tossed out. He snorted in amusement. I wasn't joking though. I was serious. His smile began to slip when I didn't laugh along. The flight attendant came through with the drink cart. I waved him off as did Mason. Handing out drinks wasn't a good sign. Landing delays sucked. Generally. Maybe this one would work to my advantage. Because now that I'd said it, I found I really wanted Mason to live with me. Once the cart was gone, I leaned back into the aisle. Mason was still gaping at me, his phone clutched in his hand.

"You weren't serious were you?" he asked in a whisper. I glanced at Eli napping in front of his brother, his ballcap pulled down low on his brow.

"As a heart attack."

He began chewing on the inside of his cheek. "Xander, that's totally insane. We've only been a couple for what? Eight days? Nine?"

"Yeah, around there but we're not the typical couple, Mason. We know each other. And not just in the biblical sense." He was shaking his head. "Don't get locked into denial. Just hear me out. We've lived together or close enough to count. I know everything about you."

"Not everything," he weakly argued.

"Please. I know you squish the pimentos out of olives then toss them on my slice of pizza. I know you squeeze the toothpaste from the middle. I know you cannot watch anything scary hence the monster on the plane wing and spacey kook freak-outs."

"Spooky Space Kook and he was terrifying."

"Sure he was. I know what music you like, what shows you record, what flavor chips you adore. There's nothing that'll surprise me about you since I've known you my whole damn life. Move in with me."

"Xander, this is insane. No, I can't. It's too soon. Everyone will say it's too soon."

I took his hand, the one without the phone, and held it tight. "To hell with what people'll say. We know we love each other. We know we can spend lots of time together. I used to be at your house or you at mine every damn day. Weekends, vacations, hockey camps."

"The hockey camps were you and Eli."

"Okay, I'll give you that, but we camped out all the time. Slept in the same tent, drank out of the same water canteens. Hell, we used to share chewing gum."

"Yeah, that was gross."

"It was but we were kids. The point is that we know each other. We're years ahead of most people in terms of discovery. There's really nothing left for us to find out because we already know it. Why spend time driving to each other's places? Paying rent and utilities?"

"I'd pay for my share at your place," he said, and it was right then that I knew I had him hooked.

Now I just had to reel him in. My heart was thumping madly in my chest. This was so right. I knew it. Deep down in my marrow having Mason in my home and life and bed was where my future lay.

"Of course. We'll work all that out. Just think though."
I gave his hand a squeeze and stared right into his soul.
"Waking up with each other every day. What we had in
Aruba we can have in Boston. We can make this work. I
know we can. We love each other so much. Move in
with me."

He seemed to be searching for something in my eyes.
His reply was slow in coming. I held his hand as we made
another loop of Logan.

"It *would* look more professional if I wasn't living in a
pool house."

"Yeah, it would. My place is perfect for a new
businessman. We can invite people over for dinner parties.
Everyone is always impressed." That was no lie. My place
was worth a cool two point four million. It was a double
townhouse, south facing, close to Public Garden, a tree-
lined street, and had been decorated by the internationally
known but Boston living designer Sacha Zhao. The cost of
having Sacha do the place nearly cost me what I'd paid for
the house but it was really stunning. Empty though. But if
Mason moved in life and light would burst from the
windows to warm the neighborhood. "There's plenty of
room. We can take one of the three bedrooms and make it
into a home office for you. You can even have your own
bath if you want. There are three and a half. Take your
pick! I know you like privacy when you're manscaping."

He blushed. "You really *do* know everything
about me."

I nodded. "Say yes, baby."

He wet his lips then nodded. I climbed out of my seat
and kissed him hard on the mouth. Within seconds, flight

attendants were hovering around me like vultures over a dead water buffalo.

"Sorry, sorry, I just had to kiss my boyfriend." I sat back down and buckled my belt. "He just agreed to move in with me."

I was beaming. Mason was red-faced. And Eli was now eyeballing me from under his Rebels ballcap. Guess he had overheard. Oh well. He could be pissy about it all he wanted. This was our life, and we were going to live it our way whether or not he or anyone else approved.

I hoped he would though.

Chapter Fourteen

Mason

I wasn't surprised when Eli stalked into my living room because he'd been lurking by the pool scowling at the pool house as if it had personally affronted him. I'd actually been waiting for him to come inside since I'd arrived at the pool house and began packing stuff into boxes. He clearly had a lot more to say about the situation, and with Xander not here it was going to be brother on brother.

"We need to talk," he announced in that tone only a big brother could get right.

"No, we don't."

"Yes, we do," he snapped, and I rounded on him.

"I think you've said enough, Eli."

He bristled and postured and then, as if his strings were cut, he slumped to the sofa and rested his arms on his knees, staring up at me.

"I don't want to argue, Mase." He sounded broken and

lost. I put down the books I'd been packing and took the chair opposite him.

"I don't want to argue either."

"It's just so fast. One minute you're my kid brother staying in the pool house, the next you're in some improbable love affair with a man I… " He shook his head then scrubbed his eyes. "I don't even know what I'm unhappy about."

My heart hurt. He'd been there for me every day he could since we'd lost our parents, he'd been my rock, my father figure, and my brother all wrapped into one. He'd encouraged me to go to college, given me a home, and he'd been part of every step of my life. From the age of sixteen, it had just been him and me against the world, and here I was, tugging on that close bond enough that if we let it, we'd never be able to fix it.

"You've done everything for me," I began, and he shook his head again as if he was denying that he had any part in me being the man I am today. "It's true, Eli. You were there for school events, every one of them when you could be, you opened your house to me—"

"You're my brother."

I sighed. "You didn't have to do any of it, Eli. You could have had your career and your life and given me money, and it would've been enough, but you didn't. When all that shit happened with Aarni, you were right there next to me, and yeah you threatened to kill him, but when you calmed down, it was you who wanted to report it all, wanted to be by my side the entire time, even if it reflected on your career."

"Mase—"

"No, listen to me for once." He made a show of zipping his lips, and I couldn't help but smile. My brother was an idiot. "Of course you're going to feel upside down about it all, and I get that, but I want you to know that I'm ready to move on, and I can only do that because of the man you helped me become."

He closed his eyes and then sniggered. "I'm responsible for that?" He waved at my scarlet and purple shorts.

"No, that's just my innate sense of style that missed you altogether."

He looked serious for a moment. "I'm going to transfer you money."

"I don't need—"

"How will you afford to pay him rent?"

"It's not like that."

"It's important that you aren't… "

"What?"

"That you hold your own, that he doesn't take advantage because he thinks you owe him."

That was what was worrying Eli? "You're talking about Xander as if you didn't know him. Jesus, Eli." I forced away the tiny niggling worries I had about my part in the finances of my new relationship. "You genuinely think that the man for whom you'd stand in front of a hundred mile puck would seriously mess with me?"

"I don't want you to end up resenting… look, I just want it to work, okay? You're so perfect for each other"— he held up a hand to stop me from talking— "but I want you to know that if something happens, if it doesn't work out, then I'd choose you. Okay? You're my brother, and I love you, and you'll always come first in my life."

I stared at him for a moment, seeing the raw emotion in Eli's eyes. It would kill him not to have his best friend in his life, but yeah, at the end of it all it was Eli-Mason against the world.

We both stood and found each other in a big hug that lasted a long time, and I knew in my heart that we'd mended something here. We'd always be brothers, and that was all that mattered.

"Which box first?" he asked, after clearing his throat and picking up the nearest box of books as if it weighed nothing—one of the benefits of being related to a man who could bench-press the weight equivalent of a small car.

"I'm just piling everything on the driveway, Xan will be here in ten."

"I'm already here," Xan said from the door. I didn't know how long he'd been there, and what he might've heard, but his glance flicked to Eli. He looked uncertain—not an expression I was used to seeing from Xander.

Eli pointed a finger at him. "If you hurt him—"

"I won't."

Eli shoved him, and Xander shoved back, which led to the two big men rolling on the ground outside the door and ending up in the pool.

"My iPhone, you fucker!" Xander yelled.

"Serves you the fuck right!" Eli yelled back.

Then the two of them collapsed in laughter, not letting either out of the pool and in the end, I gave up and let them get on with it.

Idiots.

I couldn't stop smiling though because the two men I loved might be idiots, but they were *my* idiots.

SOMETHING WASN'T RIGHT.

I hadn't given any thought to the inside of the office, caught up in company issues and finances, but I'm sure this wasn't the practical setup that we'd organized. We had three rooms in the shared building in Quincy, an old, weathered building that came complete with parking and a rent lower than downtown. One room, this room, was our back office with a small kitchen, then we had a consultation room and a family room. We'd spent all our money on the people facing rooms, and this back room was supposed to be utilitarian, and nothing like what I was looking at.

"I didn't order this," I muttered and stared at the two large solid wood desks, complete with space-age chairs, copious shelving, printers plural, computers, and at least five boxes of what looked to be assorted stationery. Photo frames were propped up against the wall, there was even a water cooler in the corner. "Who the fuck… ?"

"Wow," was all Becca managed as she dropped the box of files onto one of the desks. "I call this one."

I didn't care what desk I had because *this wasn't the desk we'd ordered.* I placed my box on the other desk, the clatter of pens enough to snap me back from my shock, which was when I saw the note propped up against a mug addressed to both of us. I opened the note and couldn't believe what I was reading out loud.

"Good luck, guys, not that you need it." I paused a moment and glanced around at what we had here. "Eli left the note." He must have done all this before the argument, before we fixed things, and emotion choked me at the fact he'd always had my back.

"Wow," Becca repeated. "Your brother is not just sex on legs, but he has a big heart."

I shot her a glance because she sounded all kinds of dreamy, and that wasn't like her. The last guy she'd dated had been a longtime thing that started in college but six months ago it had come to an end.

"You have a thing for Eli?" I teased.

"He's a hockey god with those thighs, and now his heart… " She stopped and blushed scarlet.

"Wait, I thought you liked Brady."

"I love Brady's hockey, but Eli… I mean, I backed off because he's your brother, but you're *doing* Xander, and maybe," she mumbled. "Is that an issue?"

What could I say? My best friend liking my brother— there was a delicious irony in all of that—and I smiled. "I'm not *doing* Xander, but no, I have no issue at all."

Becca returned the smile and winked, winding her long blond hair into a high ponytail then putting her hands on her hips and surveying the room. "You are so *doing* Xander. Now, where do we start?"

I picked up the mug the note had been propped up against and read the slogan. "I make families, what's your superpower?" I couldn't help smiling like an idiot. "Let's get ready to help make families."

We spent the entire day organizing the office, tidying the front facing spaces, scattering cushions on huge sofas in the living room, and unboxing a ton of toys and books that would be available for the kids attending meetings with their parents, plus the arcade machine that I know for sure we'd never ordered. Between us, we made a snug place surrounded by bookshelves, filled with cushions and placed the electronics in there, along with beanbags, and finally we stood back and surveyed everything.

"We have food," Xander announced from the door, with Eli hovering behind him. Both in Rebels jerseys and Xander grinning from ear to ear.

"We need to talk, *Eli Norris Kingsley*." Eli slunk into the room, looking sheepish, but there was also a hint of something else in his expression, and I knew he was proud of me. "You shouldn't have done all this."

He shrugged as if it didn't matter when *it did*. I hugged him, and then Becca hugged him too. Was it just me or did the Becca/Eli hug last that much longer? Also, was my superstar brother always this much of a dork around girls? He blushed scarlet and patted her shoulders when he let her go and then stumbled over his words like an idiot. He'd never done that before, not in the six years they'd known each other. We sat on beanbags, talked plans, and laughed, long into the evening. I snuggled into Xander's side and took detailed notes of how close Becca and Eli were sitting.

"I saw you looking," Eli murmured as we rinsed mugs at the sink. Xander and Becca had stayed on the beanbags and from the pointed glances between Becca and Eli, I had the feeling I was going to be hit with *news*.

"At what?" I played innocent.

"She said I needed to tell you first before I did

anything." He went scarlet again. "I don't mean… sex… "
He lowered his voice on the last word and glanced back at
the room where we could see Xander and Becca looking at
something on Becca's phone. Probably the photos from the
vacation that Dunny had uploaded en masse to our chat
group.

I fake clutched pearls and gasped. "Sex?"

He thumped my arm and it hurt. Seriously, does he not
remember I'm not a hockey player?

"I asked Becca to go out for dinner, or something, not
sex, just talking."

"Are you and Becca a new thing?"

He blushed again and dipped his head, drying the mug
so hard I'm surprised the logo didn't wear off. "No, I mean
I didn't tell her, but I've liked her since I first met her.
Only she was with that idiot Harvey, and then there was
the whole Xander-and-you 'thing,' and I thought, hell, why
not."

"Look after each other," I murmured. "Make it work so
I get to keep my best friend. Yeah?"

He wrinkled his nose at me then burst into song. "Isn't
it ironic… " Thankfully, shoving a tea towel in his mouth
was enough to stop that because neither of the Kingsley
brothers were born with an ear for staying in tune. We
headed out, with Eli offering Becca a lift, even though her
car was *right there.* I couldn't get the damn song out of my
head even after a shower and athletic sex that left me
boneless.

"Do you think it's ironic that my best friend has a thing
for my brother?" I mused as I cuddled into Xander's side.

"Yeah," was all Xander said. "It kind of is."

AMANDA MCCARTHY-DENNING WAS BOSTON ROYALTY. As the oldest daughter of a family who owned hotels, she had money, and her wife, Louise, was a former model turned actress. They'd married in a beautiful open air ceremony two years ago that'd made it onto the news. The fact that the McCarthy-Dennings had chosen the Kingsley-Clarke agency for their surrogacy journey was a feather in our cap, but they were also our first real new clients. One week into being live for business we'd mostly been dealing with clients who'd followed us from the Franklin Agency, but this was something very different.

The meeting had been set outside office hours. There was a bodyguard who loitered inside the main door, and there was an air of money about them that made my skin prickle. Neither Becca nor I were worried when their first demand was for absolute discretion. We didn't even balk at the non-disclosure paperwork. That was a familiar thing for us, particularly when dealing with high-profile clients. We signed at the relevant points without question. They'd brought a lawyer with them, a thin man with round glasses who'd stayed silent so far, but after the non-disclosure was signed, he was the one who collected the paperwork and slid it into his briefcase.

The meeting consisted mainly of the McCarthy-Dennings explaining what they wanted out of the journey, and I thought Becca and I provided a professional explanation for each step. First, they would need to check out the information we had on each donor, which was connected to another company that dealt with that side of things. The only thing they were worried about with that was the fact that a third party was dealing with what they called the *sticky* side of the situation.

"Can you assure us of their discretion?" was the cornerstone question.

"We worked directly with the medical support when we were with Franklin Agency," Becca reassured and handed out the glossy brochure full of information about surrogacy from the third party. "You can look through the options and tell us what level you'd like to sign up to. Options such as connecting with the donor and the legal side of contact after."

"We don't want that." Louise looked fearful, and Amanda took her hand.

"We want this baby, or babies, to be completely beyond any legal action. As you can understand there is a huge financial incentive there for anyone with a connection to us to want some of it and use any potential child as leverage."

"Completely," I said. "And that's the full service Kingsley-Clarke will provide in conjunction with your own legal team." I exchanged nods with their lawyer, and that seemed to be enough to reassure them.

"We have something else that's a potential issue… " Amanda paused. "Certain photos have come to our notice, and although we appreciate that you're part of the queer community, Mr. Kingsley, we can't help but have certain reservations."

"Photos?" I asked, although my stomach was already hollowing. Was this a college thing? Becca and I'd never been the hard partying kind, not even at college, but there was probably evidence of parties from when we were young. Only none of them would cause reservations, surely.

The lawyer unclipped his briefcase and handed over two photos, blown up to letter size, and I recognized them immediately from a rowdy walk on the beach, taken by Eli and shared on social media, of me and the other guys on the vacation. There was nothing indiscreet there, just a group of guys pulling faces and acting like goofs. Yes, we were all only in shorts, but we'd been swimming, and yes, I was on Xander's shoulders, but we'd been messing about. There was nothing out of the ordinary there. Oh wait, was that Dunny? Shit. He was flashing his bare white ass in the photo and I'd never noticed.

"We understand you are in a relationship with the hockey player Xander Holden." The lawyer wasn't looking for a yes or no.

"I am."

"We have concerns… " he said and glanced at Amanda and Louise. "About your partner's *celebrity* and photos such as these, being connected with my client."

"I can assure you that every step of your journey will be supported with absolute discretion," Becca confirmed. I was glad it was her that spoke as I felt a hundred kinds of awkward. The kind of clients we were attracting would be coming to us from places like the older stuffier Franklin Agency, and maybe they were right to worry that I'd be part of the celebrity culture with gentle idiots like Dunny with his lack of filter. If they only knew how much I didn't want any part of being in the media or becoming public property in any way.

We shook hands after some more discussion over timescales and the kinds of services Kingsley-Clarke would give them, but I must admit I was rattled by the veiled suggestion that a lack of moral character would lead to the client's privacy being put in jeopardy.

Was that something we should be thinking about? What level of moral character was going to be acceptable for this company to work? I thought we could start a new way of looking at surrogacy, a responsible effective and discrete service but also different to the old ways from places like the Franklin Agency who were blatantly unsupportive of same-sex surrogacy and adoption.

Was I fooling myself that my clients would want a more relaxed approach? Maybe some of them actually liked the fact that the Franklin Agency were so stuck in the past about most things. If they got the job done, then would clients put up with the passive aggressive bullshit that was dished out to same sex couples there?

I scrubbed my eyes as exhaustion swept over me.

Becca sighed and peered at the picture. "I didn't realize Dunny was uhm…"

"Me neither."

She frowned at me. "Maybe they have a point, we should get these photos untagged from you."

I wanted to argue that this didn't affect what our new company was able to offer, but it probably did.

Shit.

Chapter Fifteen

Xander

I WAS STANDING OUT IN THE BLAZING SUN ON A neighborhood baseball diamond in Roxbury surrounded by seven kids in cute little baseball shirts, pants, hats, and cleats. All provided by the Rebels. My team was the Scrappers and had a logo of a bulldog wearing a tricorne hat while holding a baseball bat in his jowls. I'd given them and their parents a short speech and had set up the tee at home base. We had a half hour of practice before the next team had the diamond.

"Okay, so I want each of you to take a turn hitting the ball off the tee," I said. They all nodded aside from Penelope, who was drawing in the dirt. She was the youngest on the team at age four. We had four boys and three girls ranging from six down to Penelope. All were inner city youth and eager to play. Well, maybe Penelope not so much, but she'd get into it. "Cory, you go first."

I stood back after placing the ball on the plastic stand.

The ball was smaller than a standard baseball and lighter. There was no pitching in tee-ball. The kids hit the ball off the stand. We'd teach them the basics of the game, but it was just a fun way to spend some time. Or that was how I'd come into it. A few of the parents seemed to think their kids were trying out for the Red Sox or something.

Cory took a swing and missed. Then cried. Wow. Okay, that was unexpected. His mother and I talked to him and calmed him down by assuring him he had more than one swing. Once his tears were dry, he tried again. And again. Fourth time was the charm though, and he hit it off the stand with a pop. We all clapped. Cory ran to third base. This team would need work, but we had all summer. I smiled down at Cory's mom, Anita, and asked her on the spot if she'd like to be the team mom.

She readily accepted so she'd be in charge of all the paperwork, signing up other volunteers, turning in the financial forms, and answering questions. See, I'd done my homework since returning to Boston. I hadn't had much else to do other than read up on tee-ball rules and regs and play golf. Mason was so wrapped up in getting his agency set up that I rarely saw him, and when we did get together, he was exhausted. Not exactly the romantic relationship we'd had in Aruba, but then again, that had been a vacation. Real life was seldom as it was on a getaway.

The kids all got a turn at the tee, and I now had a pretty good idea of who could hit and who would need some work. I sent them out to catch some balls that I planned to hit to them.

A tall man with a thick beard sauntered up to me. He

was Penelope's older brother, Aaron. The age difference between the siblings was striking, but I said nothing because who was I to comment? I'd been shocked to see that the adults who'd shown up with their kids expecting Marquis had accepted me so readily. It was a pleasant surprise.

"Can I ask you a question?" Aaron enquired as I tapped the ball off the tee and waited for a kid—any kid—to make a move to try to catch it. Yeah, we needed work.

"Sure," I replied, waving at Derrick, one of the six-year-olds, to come in from left field to grab the ball sitting next to second base. He didn't see me flagging him down as he and Monica, a five-year-old, were too busy throwing grass at each other.

"So you're the Xander Holden that just came out, yeah?"

My smile faded instantly. "That's right." I braced myself for the homophobic rant to begin.

"I thought so." He folded his arms over his yellow tank top. "My friend said the Rebels are going to make you captain. Said that Brady Rowe is dead weight, too old, and too lame to stay on the team. You think a gay dude can be captain? I mean, no offense, but who's going to listen to a powder puff?"

Wow. I just... wow. "You can tell your friend that Brady Rowe is *far* from being dead weight, too old, or too lame. The man is a beast and could clean your clock and mine with ease. Also, no offense, but I'm bi, and I can command respect the same as a straight man. The point is moot because Brady is going nowhere. He plans to retire a Rebel."

He took a step back, hands up. I hadn't realized I'd sounded that snarky but good on me if I had. Fucking powder puff my ass. If I wanted, I could beat this shitter into paste with one arm tied behind my back. Not that I'd ever take a swing at anyone not on skates and asking for it, but I could show him exactly how puffy I was.

"Okay, dude, chill out. I was just asking." He sauntered back to the stands and sat down beside some guy in a Rebels ballcap.

Anita walked up to me with a bottle of cold water. "Ignore them," she whispered.

"Thanks." I took the bottle then smiled at the pudgy Black woman. "I'm afraid I got a little snappy with him."

"Serves him right for asking such an asinine question. It'd have been fun to see you knock him on his ass like you did Morton Cloy in that game against Detroit."

I snickered as I twisted the cap off my water. "You saw that game?"

"Hell yeah. I never miss a Rebels game."

She rambled on about that fight, filling me in on team stats that I didn't even know. Then she whistled the kids in, gave them cookies and fruit punch boxes, and herded them all off the diamond to a waiting city van that would take them either to their homes or a daycare. I waved at them as they boarded the van. Each child was covered in dust and wore grass stains on their knees even though not a lick of baseball had been played. I jogged around picking up balls and the tee then headed home, a bag of gear in my backseat.

I was pleased to see Mason's car parked in front of my place when I got home. Bag of sporting goods over my shoulder, I hurried inside, calling his name as I dropped the bag and toed off my sneakers by the door. He walked out of the kitchen, phone pinned between his ear and his shoulder, a platter of sliders and fries in his hands.

"That looks great," I said, kissing his smooth cheek then swiping a small cheeseburger from the plate.

He blew me a kiss then continued talking with Becca, I presumed. I chose to sit on the rolling hassock instead of the sofa as my clothes were covered with dust. Mason settled into the sofa, chatting steadily about this approval and that form, all the while yawning because I know for a fact he hadn't slept more than an hour last night. Nor the night before when I'd found him faceplanted in paperwork with a still warm coffee by his side. Still I knew he had a ton of things to get done, and if this was hockey season I'd be just as distracted. I waited and ate until it seemed the main part of the conversation was done, and I finally tapped his knee. His gaze lifted from the cold French fry in his hand to me and he blinked as if he'd only just realized I was here.

"Sorry to interrupt but can I have you for maybe ten minutes to tell you about my morning with the kids."

"Shit yes, of course. Becca, I'm going now. No, yeah, I know we still have to iron out a few thousand things, but it's Saturday and my man needs me." I felt stupid now. Immature. Like one of my tee-ball kids whining for attention. Mason said his goodbye, lowered his phone, and gave me a hangdog look. "I'm really sorry. I know I've been the worst boyfriend since I moved in. It's just that we had a Dunny situation and it's left me—"

"What Dunny situation?" What the hell had the big oaf done now?

"In some of the tagged photos from Aruba he was flashing his ass, and I know he was only fooling around but one of our clients pulled us up on it."

"Shit. I'll talk to him."

"You don't have to, I already texted him and he was cool, untagged me, deleted it all."

He leaned over to kiss me and his lips tasted salty. I liked it a lot. I cupped the back of his head, leading him around the table to my lap. His legs wrapped around my middle, his arms dangling over my shoulders. His tongue was soft, warm, and tempting as it slid into my mouth.

"Mm," I purred into the ongoing kiss. He melted into me, his fingers resting on my shoulder blades.

"I love you," he whispered, ending the kiss then reaching back to grab another slider. This one he fed to me, bite by bite, as I filled him in on the team, our team mom, and the fact that little real baseball would probably be played. "I'll be there next Saturday for sure. It's the first game, right?"

"Yeah, we only have a few practices this week in the evening." I paused to let him place a fry between my lips. I loved the feel of him in my arms, the weight of him on my thighs. "One of the adults there asked me about Brady."

"Ah, the trade rumors." He fed me another fry.

I chewed and nodded. "Yeah. It felt as if he was trying to jab at me without sounding like a true homophobe. He asked me if I thought a gay man could be a good captain because who would listen to someone *like me*."

His jaw dropped. "No, he did not say that."

"Yeah, he did. It pissed me right the fuck off."

"As well it should have. You'd be a great captain. The whole team looks up to you." He snuggled in closer, letting his head rest on my shoulder as his fingers slid up into my hair.

"I'd be the first." I rested my cheek on his head. "Tennant Rowe doesn't have the captaincy. None of the other queer players that I know of do. I'd be the first. But it's not even worth talking about as Brady is going nowhere. The team will keep negotiating with him and then right before training camp they'll give him what he wants and that'll be that."

"Exactly. So fuck that guy and his stupid shit." He dropped a kiss to my throat.

We sat there on the hassock for a bit, saying nothing just me sucking up comfort from his closeness.

"Let's go out tonight." He lifted his head from my shoulder to look at me with surprise. "What? We've not really gone out as a couple since Aruba. Let's get dressed up and hit the town. Let's rent a sailboat. They have those romantic tours around the harbor. Oh! Or we could check out the rose garden over by Fenway. You like flowers. Then we could go to dinner somewhere chic, maybe hit a few clubs, or see a play. I bet I could get us tickets to a play at the Charles Playhouse. You said you wanted to see *Hamilton*. Oh hey, let's check out that new gay dance club on Tremont Street. You know the one. It was on the news the other night and you commented on it. How cool it looked. Let's do dinner and go dancing."

"Sure, yeah that all sounds great but," he yawned so hard his jaw cracked. "I'm so damn tired." I gathered him close, tight, and claimed his mouth hungrily. He clung to me like a vine, his kisses were sweet yet pained.

"Dinner and a play as soon as you're settled in the new company," I said.

"Thank you. I love you so much, Xander. You. Me. Us… it's just shitty timing."

I swept him up and carried him to my bed. We tumbled into bed mouths locked, hands roaming eagerly. He was a writhing live wire under me, his pleas steamy puffs of hot air fanning over my face. I got him bared with speed then licked wet stripes all over his body. I tongued his navel, his sides, his thighs, his ankles. I sucked on his toes then moved up to his weeping cock. He bucked and whimpered until I was stripped down and pressing into him, his slick heat enveloping me, the feel of his flesh tight around mine stole my breath. We'd ditched the condoms a week ago after two negative tests. I'd never imagined the difference would be this soul-shattering. With a leg hooked over my shoulder, I began to pump. The sound of my grunts, his mewls, and the slick hot sound of a lubed cock moving in and out of a tight ass filled our bedroom.

"I want… to ride… you," he huffed as perspiration beaded on his upper lip. I bent down, his knee by my ear, to lick up his salty sweat then taste his mouth. He growled at the change of position, my cock bouncing off his prostate with each flick of my hips. He pushed on my chest, so I eased out then fell to my back. He was on me instantly, easing himself down on my dick, then rolling those lean hips of his. My eyes rolled back in my head with each gyration. My orgasm was upon me before I could stop it. Hands on his hips, I held him to me, pounding up into him as I pumped him full. His soft cries of pleasure joined mine. Cum spurted over my chest, thick ribbons of white dotting my belly. I rolled us over, pushed deep, and crashed my mouth over his. We rode it out joined in every way two men could be joined.

We showered and napped afterward then went at it again that afternoon with me on the bottom. We got dinner, and hugged on the sofa, watching a cast recording of Hamilton. It wasn't quite going out for dinner and theater, but we did get to see the play, holding hands as "Helpless" filled the air. Yeah, songs about his eyes kind of did me in. I was *truly* and helplessly in love.

Chapter Sixteen

Mason

WAKING UP NEXT TO XANDER ON THE FOURTH OF JULY was about the best feeling in the entire world. Knowing we were heading to Brady Rowe's house for a barbecue was the direct opposite. Both emotions warred for dominance because despite Xander's arms around me, I couldn't stop thinking that this was the first time I couldn't avoid seeing Tennant Rowe. Not being a player or significant other, meant I could steer clear of every other team get together if there was any chance of the youngest Rowe brother attending.

Dating Xander changed all of that because last night my sexy man told me about how proud he was that finally he'd be true to himself at a team event walking in with his boyfriend holding his hand.

I'd cycled through a few plans that ranged from faking flu right through to faking a need to have to work on the Fourth. But goddammit, when he kissed me so gently, with pleasure shining in his eyes, how could I even suggest that I stay at home? Maybe today I could confront the ghosts that plagued me. If only I'd not brushed everything under the carpet. If only I hadn't been drinking? Hell, if only I hadn't dressed like I did or not made it clear I didn't want Aarni's advances.

Stop it.

"You okay there?"

"Huh?" I glanced up from where I was making a fruit loop island in milk and blinked at Xander's teasing expression.

He poured another coffee and pushed it my way. "More of the black stuff will wake you up."

"I'm not tired, I'm just… work is on my mind, is all." I winced internally at the lie and caught the moment that Xander saw right through me.

"Is it what I said about holding your hand at the barbecue? Are you worried there will be photos, maybe Dunny mooning in the background?" That last part was him teasing to get me to smile, but I was on edge about the barbecue, not the holding hands.

"No it's not that." Guilt consumed me, alongside the dread of seeing any of the Rowe boys, and I banged my forehead on the counter. Twice.

"Mase? Mase, you're worrying me." I buried my face in my arms, and he moved to lay a reassuring arm over my shoulder.

I lifted my head and sighed. "There is nothing I want more than to walk into that barbecue holding your hand and kissing you right *there* in front of the entire team. I want to kiss you in the grocery store and at the gas station.

I don't give a shit how it looks or who has their ass out in the background."

"Babe—"

"No. It's stupid. It's *all* stupid." I pulled at my T-shirt, my chest tight. "I can't even breathe."

He stood and tugged me away from the counter and headed outside, only stopping when we were by his sparkling pool and in the shade of the awning, then he pulled me close, and I buried my face into his neck, stealing all his reassuring strength. I hadn't had a panic attack like that since... forever. Not since I was cornered in that damn kitchen. My counselor, the one that Eli had demanded I go to, called it panic, and we talked our way through everything. That it wasn't my fault, that I could be the man I was and expect to get respect from people. I believed her, but it didn't mean that every so often the anxiety wouldn't sneak up on me.

"Start from the beginning."

"I never meant to tell you to stop touching me or showing everyone that you want to be with me."

"Showing people I love you," he corrected.

"That."

"And?"

"And what?"

"What else is going on? Is there a problem at work? Can I help? Am I causing issues for you—"

"No. Jesus. It's just... Ten will be at the barbecue today."

"Well, yeah, it's Brady's event. But you have to agree that even though he's a superstar, he's a nice guy, not a man who flashes his celebrity—"

"I've never actually met him."

He eased me away from him and frowned down at me. "How have you managed that? He's always visiting Boston."

"I couldn't face him, and I know it's stupid."

"Wait, is this about what happened with Aarni?"

"Mostly, yeah. I've avoided going anywhere that I might see Ten. It's a thing, is all. Me being stupid."

Now that I was calmer I took the closest chair, and I gestured for Xander to sit as well, which he did without argument. He was in a Rebels cutoff T-shirt, his hair unconstrained by gel, his face smooth of stubble and all I wanted to do was tell him that I'd never seen a man so perfect for me. His smile was gorgeous. His heart was big, and I loved him so much.

"You're not being stupid," Xander defended.

"I want to walk in holding your hand because I am so proud of us, of being in love with you. Okay? That is the easy part of this."

"Okay, but—"

"But also, I'm all messed up in my head because I want to talk to Ten, and I want his brothers to know how sorry I am that Aarni was even in a position to hurt their brother. And it has to be today because it's important to me that I'm part of your life for real. With Eli, I could avoid events. I was just the little brother, but with you, I want to be by your side, as your lover, and one day maybe your husband, your family when we have kids, so it's important that way I can go to any of the Boston events you want me to."

Xander's mouth fell open, and I felt as if I'd dropped a

bomb on him that he hadn't been expecting. Maybe I shouldn't have announced marriage and kids in such a blasé way. *I've fucked this up.*

"I'd love that," he said before I could say anything else. "Marriage I mean, and kids, one day. With you."

"You would?" I didn't mean to sound surprised, and I loved the way he chuckled.

"Always."

He reached out to take my hand and then tugged me over to straddle his lap on the huge chair, and I sank into his hold. "And I'll be right by your side when you talk to the Rowes if you want me to."

I kissed him with every molecule of love I had in my body. "I love you, Xan. So much that it hurts."

He waggled an eyebrow. "You want me to kiss it better?"

Which is how we spent way too long in bed and ended up being horribly late to the barbecue.

WE PARKED NEXT TO A LOW-SLUNG FERRARI WITH THE plate Dun1, and I patted the hood gently as we walked by. Dunny sure knew his cars and the limited edition scarlet beauty was just an example of the five or six others I knew he owned. He called them his babies, and Eli once told me he was sure the collection would grow until Dunny didn't live in a house but on a cot in the corner of a huge garage. In fact, there were a lot of fancy cars parked in the wide courtyard outside Brady Rowe's place, and all I could think was that if a car thief got past the security gates, they would have a field day.

"Okay?" Xander asked as we walked down the side of the house, following the shouts and laughter of people enjoying the day.

I slipped my hand in his and went up on tiptoes to kiss him. "Yep."

When we rounded the corner we entered into chaos, a hundred people spread out around the huge gardens, some in the pool, kids of all ages in groups dotted around, and I could name each Rebels player that had made it to the event. Dunny was the easiest one to spot. He was weightlifting two small children, much to their delight, and had an audience of adoring moms watching him. Whatever event we went to, it would always be Dunny entertaining the kids. Brady spotted us, charging over with intent.

"Guys, you made it!" He pulled Xander into an awkward sideways hug considering his sling and then did the same to me as well. Not once did I let go of Xander's hand, and it felt like the best statement I'd ever made in my entire life. Eli was there next, grumping about how late we were, but when I spotted Becca sitting with some of the other guys, I thumped him hard. Because that is what brothers did.

I didn't see Ten anywhere, but I could see his husband Jared, who was deep in conversation with one of the Rebels' coaches. In fact, I couldn't spot Jamie Rowe either, and when I saw Brady heading for a stand of trees about ten minutes after we arrived, I guessed maybe he was heading to where his brothers would be. Now might be the right time to find them together. Rip off the Band-Aid in one go. Xander and Eli were doing something by the pool, and I know Xan said he wanted to be with me, but there was a part of me that just wanted to handle this myself.

I picked up a can of soda from the big tub of ice then casually sauntered along the path at the edge of the property, the sounds of the party diminishing the further I got. I was almost to the trees when I heard someone curse loudly. Enough to stop me in my tracks.

"Bastard owner can't do that!" I wasn't sure who spoke, but it was Brady who replied. I could tell that by the strong Boston accent he had, and because I'd heard him speak in many interviews that Becca forced me to watch.

"I've only got a year left on this contract and even injured I'm worth something now if they trade me, not to mention the team cleared the cap space that my ten million a year salary clears. The Rebels need new blood, lower paid, new guys, and that's the way hockey is. We all know that." Brady was so patient, but whoever the first person was just cursed again.

"Nick Sinclair is an asshole."

"Calling the Rebels team owner names isn't helping, *Jamie*," a third voice said with added sarcasm.

So Brady *and* Jamie Rowe were there, which meant maybe that third voice was Ten. I didn't mean to eavesdrop, but this was a heated debate.

"Brady's given his entire career to Boston, and Nick *the fuck* Sinclair thinks it's a good idea to trade him out, fuck's sake, Ten, show some emotion."

"I am showing emotion," Ten snapped. "I'm as pissed as you are but shoving all of this shit at Brady isn't helping at all."

"Fuck, Ten. Why worry about our brother when you're sat okay in Harrisburg."

"What the hell is that supposed to mean?"

"You'll never find out what it's like to be traded when no one would dare to trade their darling superstar—"

"The fuck, Jamie—"

"Guys, stop arguing," Brady interrupted. "This could be good timing, okay? I'm tired, and I want to think through my options so no decisions okay. I just wanted you to know."

I backed away because the last thing they needed was to know I was close enough to hear them talking, only my heel hit a stone, and I tumbled back into a heap of bushes onto my ass into the dirt, letting out a yell as the cold soda hit the dirt and exploded in a mess of sugar and ice.

"You okay?"

I blinked up at Tennant *freaking* Rowe, who had his hand out to help me up.

"Embarrassed," I muttered and took his hand, pulled up in one go, and then Ten was brushing me down of earth and soda before he stepped back and put his hands on his hips.

"It happens to all of us," he nodded knowingly. Unspoken was the added *when you hover to listen to people's conversations.* Well shit.

"Are you okay, Mason?" Brady asked, and Jamie was there as well. In fact, I was faced with a smirking row of incredibly handsome Rowe brothers. If I wasn't so head over heels for Xander, I'd be tongue-tied right now.

"I'm good, thanks. Uhm, I'm Mason, Eli's brother," I explained to Jamie and Ten and then stopped because where did I go from there. "I wanted to talk to you," I blurted, and they looked at each other and then back at me. "You," I pointed at Ten.

Ten smiled at me in encouragement. "Okay?"

Brady and Jamie began to leave but that wasn't right. "All of you, actually."

I stalked past all three of them, right to where they'd been talking, hidden from the party, in a quiet space, and there was plenty of room for me to pace in front of them when they joined me.

"I know you're with Xander," Brady reassured me. "If that's what you're worried about. The team chat blew up with it last week, and Xander spoke to me. He seems happy and settled, and that's what I want for him as his captain and friend." Seemed to me as if Brady had rehearsed that little speech because he looked pleased with himself that he'd recalled all the right things to say.

What is wrong with me? Brady is a good guy. He's not rehearsed anything at all.

"Thank you, but it's not about Xander." I stopped my pacing. Maybe I should have waited for Xander to find me. I could have done this with his steady presence next to me. "It's about Aarni Lankinen."

Ten stiffened, Jamie cursed, and Brady's smile slipped, his eyes narrowing. None of them said a word.

"What did he do now?" Jamie growled.

"No, not now, this was a long time ago, when I was younger. It was my eighteenth birthday, his team was in town, and there was a thing at my brother's place the other team had been invited to. Aarni cornered me, in the kitchen, and after a while I didn't like it, but I couldn't get away." Words failed me.

"Fucker," it was Brady's turn to growl. Ten took a step toward me, his face a mask of compassion.

"I'm so sorry," he murmured, but I didn't want sympathy.

"I didn't tell anyone." I took a step away and collided with something hard. *Someone hard.* A man who put their arms around me and held me tight. I hadn't even heard Xander approach, but I knew it was him and from the way he held me he was probably in full-on protector mode. "Eli and Xander wanted to kill him, then they wanted to report him, but I wouldn't let them," I ended miserably. "Aarni had been flirting with me, and I'd had a beer, and I was flattered at first, and then I didn't move out of his way. It was half my fault."

"Bullshit," Xander and Jamie said at the same time.

"If I'd had the balls to say something to the cops, or his team, then Aarni might have been watched, or fired, or… all I know is, he wasn't, and he went on to hurt others, and then you. Ten, he hurt you, and I'm so sorry, but maybe I could have stopped it all."

Ten took a step closer to me, but Xander held me tight, and even though I couldn't move I felt protected. Ten didn't look angry, in fact, he seemed resigned and sad. He reached out to touch my arm then gripped me and tugged me from Xander's hold. Xander released me until I was pulled into a hug with Ten.

"Not your fault," Ten murmured into the fierce hug. "You were as much a victim as the rest of us, I promise you it wasn't your fault. Please don't tell me you've been carrying this with you all this time."

I wanted to do something stupid, like cry, or hug Ten back, or ask him to punch me, or something because my skin felt too tight, and I couldn't reach Xander.

"I should have said something," I murmured against Ten's neck, and he hugged me closer, holding me as tight as Xander had done.

"Nah, it wouldn't have fixed a damn thing," Ten said then eased me away. I was immediately pulled into a hug by Jamie then Brady. Xander waded into the Rowe hugathon and pulled me free and held my hand.

"Okay, so we're cool here?" Xander asked, but his shoulders were back, and he was primed for confrontation, bristling with all the love he had for me. I cuddled into him, never loving him more than I did at this moment, never feeling more protected or ridiculously over-loved in return.

"It's all good," Ten said with a wide smile, patting my arm. "You know where I am if you ever need to talk."

"And me," Jamie added, with his own pat.

"Likewise." Brady nodded.

I felt as if the most enormous weight had been lifted. Not because I didn't carry survivor's guilt or because I could stop playing devil's advocate on how I might have changed what happened to Ten and the others. It was because the words and fears were out in the open, and nothing was as soul-destroying when it was out in daylight.

"I'm hungry," Jamie announced. "I need food." He

headed up the path, with Ten following close, but when Xander started to leave, Brady stopped him.

"Can we talk, Xan?" He sounded so serious, and I knew this was going to be hockey related, and like Jamie, I was all of a sudden very hungry.

"I'll see you up there." I wrapped my arms around Xander's neck and kissed him hard then headed up the path with the others. Ten was waiting, slinging his arm over my shoulder, and telling me a story about the Railers' goalie and a mouse.

And everything felt right.

Chapter Seventeen

Xander

Brady led me indoors and into the kitchen.

"Soda?" he asked as he tugged open the fridge then tossed a can at me. The kitchen looked like a cyclone had blown through it but that was to be expected. Lisa was feeding a hundred people. The woman was amazing. "Sorry. It's diet. Lisa's on this weight loss thing." He popped the tab with a hearty sigh.

"Diet is fine."

"I hate diet soda," he lamented then drained half the can. I opened mine, took a sip, and then reached down to pet Bourque who was cleaning up crumbs. A canine Roomba. "Okay, so I wanted to talk to you in private about this."

"Oh-kay." I could feel an impending doom moving into the room like a low fog.

"I think they're going to trade me."

I shook my head. "Nope. Won't happen. You're the team captain. They won't trade you."

Brady smiled into his soda can. "My friend, they traded Gretzky." Okay yeah, they did. But my point still stood. Brady Rowe *was* Boston hockey. He fucking lived and breathed this team and this town. "My agent just called me before the party started. Sinclair said that they'd be willing to let me stay at a diminished capacity for one year with a pay cut."

"What? What the *fuck* does that even mean?" The dog looked up at my loud outburst. I reached down to pet his soft head.

"It means they want me to sit on the bench and impart wisdom to all the young kids they're going to bring in to replace me." His brow furrowed as he stared into his can. "Which is utter bullshit." His green eyes lifted from his soda to me and the pain I saw in them gutted me. Fucking Sinclair is doing this to him. I mean I knew we were nothing but commodities, living breathing stocks and bonds to be shuffled and sold off when our worth began to dip a bit, but this kind of shit sucked. "I'm not willing to do that. I either play balls to the wall or I leave now with some dignity."

My head was full of whirling thoughts and feelings. The dog woofed lightly in greeting. I craned my head to see who was coming in while taking a sip of soda to wet my whistle. I nearly choked when I saw the team owner standing in the doorway.

"The little lady told me I could find you here," Nick said then walked into the room as if he owned the place. I glowered at him. "Xander, can Brady and I have a moment?"

I opened my mouth to tell the *Miami Vice* knockoff to go fuck himself when Brady chimed in. Which probably saved me from being traded to Siberia. Who the hell wears a pink shirt with white shorts other than Crockett and/or Tubbs?

"Xander is one of my best friends and my defensive partner. He knows me better than my wife. I just told him about the impasse that we're at." He tossed his can into the sink where the remaining soda poured out, fizzing its way down the drain. "Why are you even here? Shouldn't you be talking to my agent about this?"

"Yeah, probably but he was getting on my nerves. Guy's like a chihuahua with a rectal malady." That was Nick. Just say what's on your mind. "Fucking snipping and barking. I like to talk face to face with the people I'm doing business with."

Brady exhaled deeply, eased his freshly rebuilt shoulder—God knows how many times he'd had them operated on by now—and leveled a stoic stare at Nick.

"Okay then explain to me why you're offering me a shitty one year diminished responsibility contract."

"Because we need new blood. Look at our roster. Half the guys look like you." Nick waved a hand heavy with gold rings at Brady then me. I cocked an eyebrow. "Our roster is heavy with players thirty and over. We need to start making moves to bring up the young talent. I knew you'd not go quietly into the night, so this is a nice bridge contract. You spend a year with... maybe with another team, easing into retirement while passing along all your knowledge to the young guns."

Another team? The fuck!

"I hate all of those suggestions," Brady said, and I nodded in agreement.

"I figured you would. I know you have pride. I also know what the stats are telling me. We're rebuilding. Now, you can take this offer or not. Your contract is about to expire so you're free to go to some other team with our blessings. Or you can retire, and we'll find you a spot on the coaching staff. It's nothing personal. Just money."

Brady and I exchanged looks. So this rebuild was really taking place. Huh. And the coaches were getting the chop just like some of the players. Nothing new there. Coaches were usually cannon fodder when a team was slipping in production.

Nick nodded, his ebony hair catching glints of the overhead lights. "You should talk to your wife. Women tend to get upset when their husbands make decisions unilaterally. Been there and done that. So, you and your lovely bride ponder on your future."

"We don't need to talk," Lisa said from behind us. I wonder how much she'd heard, but just the sound of her voice made Brady visibly relax. "We've already decided."

She came to stand next to her husband, and Brady pulled her into his side, holding her close.

"I'm retiring," Brady announced, and not one of us said a thing. This was the end of a partnership for me that had been the making of me as a player. Brady not wearing the C was something I never thought I'd have to deal with. But he stared at me, and there was a peace in his eyes that

I'd never seen before. I bet he'd cried over this, and railed at the hockey gods for his injuries, but for his family, he'd chosen to stop.

I admired the hell out of him, extending my hand which he took in a sharp shake.

"Fuck, Brady," I said with feeling.

"Yeah," was all he said back before he pressed a smiling kiss to Lisa's head. "It was time." Then he put some distance between his wife and himself and stared at Nick. "I have something else to say."

"This is my cue to leave," Lisa murmured, and we all politely smiled as she left, waiting for whatever Brady was going to say that had him looking so serious.

"Xander should be captain." He tilted his chin in defiance, expecting for Nick to argue. "I know the team management has to have their eyes on him. He's got considerable leadership capability, has been with the team for several years, the men respect him, and he's got a cool head on the ice. He'd be a perfect choice."

Nick's dark eyes flickered to me then back to Brady.

"He's queer," Nick blurted out as if that were something bad. My eyes narrowed as did Brady's.

"Excuse me," I said since Brady seemed to be dumbstruck as well as pissed. "Are you saying that because I'm bi I'd not be a good captain for this team?"

Nick exhaled dramatically. "Got any scotch in that thing?" He jerked a thumb at the fridge. Brady shook his head. Outside the squeals of children could be heard. "I never said you wouldn't be a *good* captain. I just said you're queer and that makes things trickier."

"How the hell can you stand there and spout such

bullshit?" Brady snapped. The dog slunk out of the kitchen, poor old sod. I'd have to sneak him a bite of hot dog later. "You yourself stood in front of the team not that long ago and said you slept with men."

"Yeah, I did and yeah I do, but I'm not the captain. I'm the owner. I drive too fast. I drink too much scotch. I smoke imported Cuban cigars, and I dress in what many would call South Palm Beach Retro. No one cares what I do. The fans could give two shits if I fucked llamas."

I wanted to argue. Really I did but the bastard had a point. Players were held up to a different standard, and captains were even more rigorously vetted.

"This is stupid," Brady interjected. "The fact that he's into guys should have no bearing. My brother Ten—"

"Isn't the Railers captain," Nick quickly threw out. And there it was, the fact of the moment, lying on the counter next to a dirty cake pan. "Look, I'm not saying it's right. To be honest, it sucks big hairy balls. But this is the world we live in at the moment. The fans are still trying to adjust to there being a bisexual man on the team. Two if you count your cousin who's pretending to be discreet but is seen all over town with his barista boyfriend. I just saw the pictures he shared on Instagram from their little trip to Disney World. Nothing like two queers in mouse ears to spark the hearts and likes from the female fans."

Austin and Robbie. Yeah, they weren't exactly being super discreet. And I could understand that completely. I wasn't hiding my boyfriend either. Fuck that. I was out and proud and loved Mason dearly.

"As the diversity rep—"

Nick waved a hand at Brady. "You don't have to go

there. I know. I know. I'm just saying that the Railers aren't stupid. Yes, Tennant and Xander are great alternates. Yes, they should get the C for their sweaters. I'm just not sure this is the proper time for management to choose a bisexual man for such a coveted position." Brady and I both started mouthing off. Nick, all five foot seven of him talked over our robust protests. "Would you two shut the hell up? Jesus loves my sweet mother you guys make my life a roller skate."

"What does that even mean?" I enquired.

"It's something my mother says." Ah so a Greek saying. That didn't clear up a thing. "It's like nothing ever goes steady or easy with this team. I'm always on my ass with the wind knocked out of me." I glanced at Brady, who was just as befuddled as I was by the looks. "Now that I can speak I'll finish. Picking a new captain will be turned over to the team to choose who leads them."

Brady's mouth dropped. I blinked as if I'd collided with a rhino.

"But we've never let the team pick. Ever since the inception of this team back in 1924. The captain has always been chosen by management," Brady stated.

"Yeah well, new times and all that. We have to be more willing to bend and change. I suspect that if the team chooses you as their captain, the hue and cry from the small but vocal homophobe squad will be lighter." Nick threw me a look. "As for you, keep doing what you're doing. The press hasn't had a damn bad thing to say about you and we want to keep it that way. Now where's the bar?"

"It's a dry party," Brady informed Nick. "We have kids here."

"For fuck's sake," Nick grumbled. Off he went into the night muttering about the lack of a bar at a team party. Brady and I stood in the kitchen, staring at each other.

"Do you feel as if you've just been run over by a tank?" I asked and he nodded. What must it be like to be so certain on the future? Was there life after hockey? Of course there was, but to get there was the most difficult of decisions. "What are you going to do next?"

"Next? I'm going to go find my wife, kiss her on the cheek, and spend the rest of the night with my friends and loved ones. I suggest you do the same."

I couldn't imagine the Rebels without Brady. "But what about the decision about coaching—"

"It's just a game, Xan. There are more important things than hockey."

"Who are you and what have you done with Brady Rowe?"

He chuckled in what sounded like resignation. "I'm still here. Just an older and sorer version of that young man you met all those years ago."

"You're still the biggest, baddest asshole on the ice."

His lips quirked. "Thanks. You're a big asshole as well. Let's go find our other halves."

THAT NIGHT, WELL AFTER MIDNIGHT, I WAS LYING IN BED with Mason

It was hard to pin down what kind of mood I was in. Part of me was saddened to still be in this place where queer people had to tiptoe around. Yes, we'd made progress. Lots of it. But damn there was such a long way to go.

"Did you see the latest IG update from Marquis?" Mason asked as he scrolled through social media one last time before we turned out the lights. I had a book I was supposedly reading on my Kindle, which was propped up on my chest. I'd read the same line at least twenty times by now.

"No, I didn't see it." I'd not checked my phone other than for messages since we'd left the party. Too much on my mind for inane posts about what some starlet had for dinner.

"Do you even follow him?" Mason asked as he stretched out beside me, his bare body pressed tightly to my side.

"Maybe?"

His huff made me smile. "Well, he's in Monte Carlo. On a nude beach." I rolled my head to look down at him. He was smirking. "Yep, you heard me right. On a nude beach. With men all flocking around him."

"Guess he's not worried about being Mr. Conservative," I muttered then sighed.

"Not in the least. Tonight he's meeting with the crown prince of Monaco then he's jetting off to some tiny little province north of Norway. Or was it south? Well, whatever. He's out there chit-chatting with royalty and flouncing around on nude beaches being an out pan Black man. And Sinclair has the balls to tell you that you have to be above reproach. It just pisses me off. Why do you have to walk this straight and narrow path?"

"Not so straight." He rolled his eyes. "That's the catch. And I'm not walking any path, straight or queer until training camp. Right now, I'm not even sure I'd take the C if they offered it."

"Oh please, stop. You'd be so damn honored to be the team captain your buttons would burst. If you were wearing something with buttons." He chucked his phone, and the images of Marquis cavorting with crowned princes and nude French men, to the nightstand then walked his fingers down my chest.

"Yeah, you're right. And that makes me mad at myself."

"Why? You've been on the team for twelve years, you and Eli both. If anyone deserves that letter it's you. Or him. I think you because you're less prone to be a dumbass."

I chuckled. "I'm telling him you said that when we play golf tomorrow."

"Pfft. I'm not afraid of him." His fingers strayed down around my navel. My cock started to stir to life as his hand drew closer to it. "You're the natural choice."

I rolled over to press him into the mattress. He gazed at me with adoration. I lowered my mouth to his. He tasted of mint toothpaste. His hands snaked around my neck, keeping my lips tight to his.

"You're such a good kisser." He sighed when I left his lush mouth to feast on his collarbones. I suckled a dark mark on his armpit that left him breathless from a giggle fit. Then I moved down his side, kissing each rib until I reached his hip. I followed his pelvic bone to his cock then took the fat head in my mouth. He arched up, his fingers clasping at my shoulders, easing more cock down my throat. I sucked him off leisurely, taking my time until he blew to bits in my mouth. I loved the salty bitter flavor of him.

"You're good at other things too," he rasped when I moved back over him, licking my way back to his mouth.

"Am I good at loving you as you deserve?" I asked, bracing myself arms locked, my gaze grabbing his. He was mellow now. Sated and serene. "Are we doing this gay couple thing correctly? Should we be more out? Prouder? More vocal? I feel like I'm letting my queer brothers and sisters down."

He placed his hands on either side of my face, his thumbs resting on my cheekbones. "And this is why the team will vote you in as captain if Brady steps down. You always worry about everyone else first. We're doing us just fine. Are you happy?"

"Deliriously."

"So am I. So we're doing things right. Are we Marquis level? No, but that's not our life, it's his. Stop worrying over everything else."

"I'm sorry. I can't seem to shake the worry that if the guys do vote for me that I'll bring some sort of upset or division to the dressing room. Maybe they're not ready for a gay captain. Maybe Sinclair was right."

"And maybe Sinclair doesn't know you like I do." He led my mouth to his. Our tongues met and tangled. "Mm, so sweet. Are you still thinking about the Rebels?"

"Maybe?"

His nose wrinkled. It was beyond adorable. "Let me see what I can do to get your mind off hockey."

With a wink, he wiggled downward until my knees rested on either side of his head and my cock was in his mouth. He took every inch of me down his throat with greedy sounds of glee, his hands on my ass, prompting me to fuck his mouth. I studied him, the slip of my wet dick in and out of his mouth, the way his lips stretched to accommodate my girth. He hummed and slurped as I rocked my hips. Fingers splayed on the wall above the headboard, I pumped a load into his mouth. He groaned around my cock, swallowing each pulse until he had me milked dry. I collapsed backward, my dick leaving his lips with a loud POP! that made him snicker.

"Holy hell," I gasped as I lay there staring at the ceiling as my lungs worked for air. Mason slunk up over me, dropping tiny kisses along the way until his lips were on mine. I slid a hand into his hair, licking deep, my essence fresh and strong on his tongue.

"Still thinking about hockey?"

"What is this hockey of which you speak?" His laughter fell over me like a soft summer sheet fresh from the line. No matter what darkness or worry rested on my shoulders Mason eased me. I brushed some hair from his face. "Did you know I love you more than anything?"

He spread his slight weight over me as a brush of a summer breeze moved through the open window to cool us.

"I'm not sure if I do know that. Better tell me again, just to make sure."

"I love you more than anything."

"More than pizza?"

"Yeah."

"More than root beer?"

"Yeah."

"More than puppies?"

I paused to consider. "Yeah. But only just."

"Okay, that's fair. More than hockey?"

"For sure."

"Good. I love you more than anything too."

He kissed me softly and all my worries blew away on that sweet summer wind.

Epilogue

Mason

THE PAPERWORK WAS PILING UP. IT WASN'T BECAUSE I WAS ignoring it, just that we had a ton of things to wade through on the McCarthy-Denning case. There was so much on the legal side, particularly with the amount of money they had between them, and the privacy, anonymity, and trust issues, and today I'd felt as if I wasn't a family expert but a trainee lawyer. The final paperwork would go through lawyers, but for now it was us checking everything in preparation.

"Last one," Becca murmured, but she was talking to the folder not me.

I put aside the rest of my to-do list, turning my attention back to adding information to our brand new website, stupidly proud of myself for not messing it up when I dragged a photo from my desktop to the software. I even remembered to update our Instagram with the same image—score one for social media dominance. We even got two likes, but one of them was Eli, and the other Xander, so that didn't count. Of course, them liking the post meant they weren't at the diamond, which meant they'd be here soon, interrupting our day, and causing a general nuisance.

I loved every minute of Xander being in my life. I loved Xander.

Becca thumped another folder on my desk and smirked when I shot in the air. "You've got that look," she announced with her hands on her hips.

"What look."

"The one where you're thinking about Xander."

"Says the woman who was staring into space for five minutes with her coffee."

The smirk turned into a genuine smile. It appeared to me that Becca and Eli had been hiding some serious feelings of their own because outside of me and Xander, I'd never seen anyone so smitten in such a short time. The phone ringing cut short the teasing, and I answered it immediately.

"Kingsley-Clarke, Mason speaking."

"Hi, is this Kingsley's brother? The guy dating Holdy?" Great. The last thing I wanted was some fan calling the office, but I suppose we couldn't avoid it. One day when we've actually made some money then maybe we could hire a receptionist, but for now we were doing it all ourselves, and we'd fielded our share of crank calls.

"What is this concerning?" I asked evenly casting a look of exasperation at a confused Becca, who crossed her eyes at me.

"My name is uhm… Dan. Dan Bailey." The man

paused as if I should know the name, and it did seem familiar. He'd gone so quiet that I pulled the phone from my ear to check we were still connected. "I'm a single hockey player. Not NHL level like your brother and your... yeah... but I play for the Schooners, in Essex, they're a feeder team for the Rebels, you know?"

Of course I knew who the Essex Schooners were. Any kind of desire to play hockey may have passed me by, but I'd grown up around Eli and Xander, and forgotten more about the game than what most people ever knew. I recognized the guy's name, not able to put a face to him as I'd been so sunk into setting up Kingsley-Clarke, but aware he was causing a stir in the AHL. Why was he calling? Was this some kind of stupid prank call? I bristled but remained cool.

"And?"

"I don't know where to start, but I know you'd understand where I'm coming from... " More pausing. "Is this a confidential thing?"

"What thing?"

Becca and I exchanged glances, and she mouthed a *what* as Dan cleared his throat. "My best friend wants to have a baby, no, *we* want to have a baby, and I said I would, y'know, donate, but her brother is all over her to not be stupid, and he's an asshole. He keeps saying we'll both find someone to love one day, but fuck... I'm happy as I am, and Chloe, that's my friend, she's had a lot of shit happen to her. Look, I know your website is all about inclusion, and she's gay, and I'm demi, but her brother doesn't get that, and I don't understand how the surrogacy journey will work, or where we'd even start, but your agency, you could help us right?"

Everything spilled out of him so fast that I had trouble keeping up, and in the end, I pulled a notebook toward me.

"Of course we can help, how about you start from the beginning?"

By the end of the call, we had a meeting set up, and I pulled out the gold colored folders we were using for the client pack—a ton of information for someone to read through before they made a decision collated in one place —sealed it and put into the mail.

"Maybe we can just focus on the hockey market," Becca teased and sat back in her chair, feet up on the desk. "Better get some marketing out to the Railers and the Raptors."

"On it." I pretended to write a note and then huffed a laugh at the joke and rolled my shoulders. It was six. I was hungry and tired, but I'd never felt so exhilarated. I'd managed to calm down Dan, plus give him some viable and realistic options for himself and his friend, and I'd assured him that we *could* help. I'd said it with absolute confidence backed up by experience. We didn't get much of a chance to debate what had happened when the sound of two hockey players heading down the corridor had us both knowing our workday was finished.

The door flew open in the only way that Eli knew how to enter a room, with energy and determination, and he scooped Becca up and out of her chair before we even got a hello.

"I'm kidnapping you," Eli announced and kissed her soundly before they left hand in hand and all of that without a hello for his little brother. Only when the coast was clear did Xander peek around the door then saunter in with a shit-eating grin on his face.

"Hey, sexy." He leered and leaned right over my desk to steal a kiss, sighing in pleasure when I laced my fingers behind his neck and held on tight. I could kiss him forever, and even then it wouldn't be enough.

"Hey back," I said into the kiss, and when we finally broke for air, he placed a bag on the desk. I recognized the logo immediately and fell on the contents as if I was starving, only stopping to talk after I'd inhaled half the sandwich. Xander ate with more care, and he watched me the entire time with an indulgent smile.

"Did you even get lunch?" He dabbed at his lips with a paper napkin.

"No time, seriously, we're busy—two more enquiries, no three now—and lots of legwork on our latest clients. If even one of those enquiries pan out, then we'll be golden." I wanted to tell him about the conversation with Dan Bailey, but confidentiality was a real thing, and I played by the rules.

He kissed me again. "I'm so proud," he whispered against my lips. We settled back, and I finished my cheesy goodness at a more sedate pace and sipped my frosty soda after each bite. When I finished I patted my belly and stretched in my chair, aware I hadn't moved from it much since seven this morning. Becca said something about introducing yoga into our day, but that was somewhere between coffee number four and five, and we debated it for thirty seconds and decided we didn't have time.

Goal one, hire a receptionist. Goal two, get yoga mats.

He went to the bathroom, but when he didn't come back after a while I went to see if he was okay, only because of the fact that Becca had spent five minutes locked in the washroom after coffee number seven. The lock was stiff to pull, but surely that hadn't caused Xander an issue. I found him in the family room, standing in front of the huge pinboard which took up an entire wall. It was half full already with posters and photos, puzzles for kids, information for prospective and existing parents, along with a sign-up sheet for things like Lamaze classes. Honestly, we'd thought of everything and it was this entire picture of being a parent that we wanted to create, from the idea of wanting a child, to actually growing a family. I slid my arms around his waist from behind and rested my forehead on his broad back, inhaling the scent of him and feeling overwhelmingly peaceful. He turned in my hold and hugged me tight then took my hand and faced the posters again.

He sighed heavily. "Nick Sinclair called me today, reiterated what he said at the party, about me and the captaincy, and I hung up on him."

"Your team owner might be mega rich, but his money didn't buy him compassion or care. Asshole."

"He's all about money and numbers is all. I don't want to judge, but you know with his opinion on me being fit to captain the team, and then the highs of loving *you*, I want something else for our future than strangers judging what I can and can't do."

"I get that."

"Did you ever think about this?" he asked, and I

glanced up at him and saw he was staring at the large poster of two smiling men with a baby and a toddler.

"Think about having a child you mean?"

"Yeah. You know, making us into a bigger family for real, with kids, and a dog, and a minivan."

I snorted. "You in a minivan?"

He frowned at me then smiled. "I would you know. When I'm done with hockey, I'll be the best dad I know, I'll drive a van if that's what it takes."

"You're not retiring for a very long time," I reminded him.

Another sigh—as if the weight of the world was on his shoulders. "I'm thirty now. I have five useful years left, maybe less. I don't carry the injuries some of the guys do, but I don't want to face what Brady went through. I want to decide for myself when it's enough and it's time for me to go, not because I'm in pain."

"You'll know when it's right," I reassured him. "Then when you do retire, I'm one-hundred-percent wanting to create a family."

He looked thoughtful and worried at his lip, pulling it between his teeth then releasing it. "There are kids out there who need a family, I thought a lot about maybe adopting."

"You did?"

"I'd reached the point where I knew you were what I needed, the man I loved… " He stopped and smiled down at me. "I knew I wanted a family, and I thought about some of the kids I teach, and how adopting a child that age might be what I was meant to do. What do you think about that? Is that something you can see us doing?"

I leaned into him and he put an arm over my shoulder, pulling me into his side.

"Yes. And we could start with fostering when things are settled with your career and with the business here."

"For real?"

My heart expanded with love, and I tugged him down to my height until we were eye to eye.

"Forever might get lonely if it was just the two of us," I murmured. "Let's make the biggest brightest family we can, get twenty dogs, and a minivan each because I want it all with you."

We hugged and then stared at the poster in silence, our fingers interlaced.

"I wish I'd been able to be honest before—we lost so much time." There was real pain in his voice, and I wasn't going to let him think about what might have been when we had the rest of our lives together. So I jumped him, caught him off balance, and tumbled my big bad hockey player back onto the sofa, pinning him to the cushions and kissing him until he didn't have the capacity to have any regrets.

"I love you," he muttered fiercely and twisted his fingers in my hair, holding me still for more kisses.

Love, life, and a family with the man who stole my heart?

Bring it on.

WANT TO READ LOST IN BOSTON, AUSTIN & ROBBIES Boston Rebels love story prequel for free? Lost in Boston available here

Next for the Rebels

Back Check (Rebels 2)

Meeting Joachim could save his daughter's life, but it may well cost Isaac his heart.

It's been one hell of a year for Joachim Löfgren. After a long summer in rehab, he's been moved to a new town, one far away from the warm Florida sun he so adores, to bolster a struggling Boston defense since the departure of their beloved team captain. He hasn't even unpacked his skates properly when fate lands another blow, and he's told that he is dad to a gravely ill child he never knew existed. It's an easy decision for the burly defenseman to help and he opens up his new home to his child and her guardian Isaac. He's instantly enchanted with the preschooler as well as her uncle and decides that his life will only be complete if his daughter is part of it. Filing for custody is the only option he feels he has, but this throws his budding relationship with Isaac into utter chaos. The two men soon find themselves on opposite sides of the courtroom as they both fight for the life they feel is best for Sophia.

Despite grieving for the loss of his sister, Isaac doesn't hesitate to take on the responsibility for his newborn niece Sophia, creating a brand new family of two built on love and laughter. He has a steady income painting pet portraits during the day, but it's the subversive and satirical cartoons he draws at night that silence his thoughts in the dark. They don't have much as a family, but he is Sophia's dad now, and nothing and no one will ever come between them. When a routine pediatric checkup shows that Sophia is ill, it forces Isaac to confront every one of his fears. Finding a matching donor is her only hope, and Isaac begins the journey to find Sophia's mysterious father. There are no names or dates in his sister's battered journal, and all Isaac knows is that he's looking for a hockey player who was nothing more than a one night stand. Little does he know that finding Joachim could destroy everything.

Hockey Series' from RJ Scott & V.L. Locey

Harrisburg Railers

Owatonna U Hockey

Arizona Raptors

Boston Rebels

LA Storm

Chesterford Coyotes - Young Adult

Free Reads

Please note - in all of these free stories, there will be some
spoilers for the main series books.

Railers Short Stories

Volume 1 | Volume 2

LA Storm

Sparkle

The Colts - AHL Short Stories

Pucks & Percentages

Breakaway

Making the Save

Standalone

Waiting for Christmas

Harrisburg Railers

When hockey wunderkind Tennant Rowe meets his new coach, he knows he's in trouble. Jared Madsen is nine years older than Tennant, impossibly attractive, and — worst of all — his brother's off-limits best friend. Is their chemistry worth the risk?

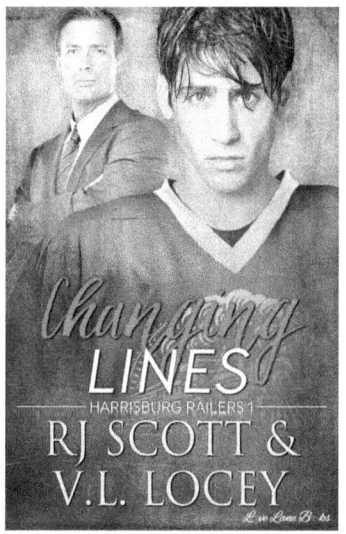

Changing Lines (Railers 1)

Can Tennant show Jared that age is just a number, and that love is all that matters?

The Rowe Brothers are famous hockey hotshots, but as the youngest of the trio, Tennant has always had to play against his brothers' reputations. To get out of their shadows, and against their advice, he accepts a trade to the Harrisburg Railers, where he runs into Jared Madsen. Mads is an old family friend and his brother's one-time teammate. Mads is Tennant's new coach. And Mads is the sexiest thing he's ever laid eyes on.

Jared Madsen's hockey career was cut short by a fault in his heart, but coaching keeps him close to the game. When Ten is traded to the team, his carefully organized world is thrown into chaos. Nine years his junior and his best friend's brother, he knows Ten is strictly off-limits, but as soon as he sees Ten's moves, on and off the ice, he knows that his heart could get him into trouble again.

Changing Lines

Harrisburg Railers (Hockey Romance)

Railers Volume 1 | Railers Volume 2 | Railers Volume 3 | Railers Volume 4

`

Owatonna U, College Hockey

Meet the men of Owatonna University's hockey team

Ryker (Owatonna U, 1)

Ryker

**Ryker is hockey royalty, Jacob is a poor country boy. Can two
vastly different people find common ground and become the
men they want to be?**

Ryker comes from a long line of championship-winning hockey
players. Playing college hockey to develop his game is his only
focus, and nothing will stand in the way of him working to

become the best player. He has no room for relationships, people who point out his flaws, or anyone who calls him on his dreams. He certainly has no place for love, and meeting Jacob is nothing but a useful distraction on the side. After all trying to get his Owatonna Eagles teammate into bed is less work and more play. When tragedy rocks his family, his charmed life crumbles, and the only person he can turn to is the same one who claims to hate him.

Jacob Benson has only known hard work and stifling conservative values his whole life. Born and raised in the small rural community of Eden Crossing, Minnesota, he's the only son of a hard-working but struggling dairy farming family. Jacob is using his skills in hockey to finance his way to an agricultural science degree. These four years at Owatonna U. will probably be the only time he has to enjoy life, gain acceptance about his sexuality, and live openly before his inevitable return to the farm. Running into a pretty rich boy like Ryker Madsen is putting a damper on his enjoyment of life away from home. Ryker's flip, conceited, carefree attitude grates on Jacob's every nerve. So why, if Ryker is everything he dislikes, does he want nothing more than to explore the sinful dreams that his annoying teammate stars in every night?

Ryker

Owatonna U Hockey (Hockey Romance)

Arizona Raptors

Coast to Coast (Arizona Raptors 1)

Coast To Coast

When opposites attract, this bottom-of-the-league team will never be the same again.

A stipulation in his father's will forces Mark back into the arms of a family that disowned him and leaves him one-third owner of a hockey team facing financial ruin. He doesn't even watch hockey, let alone like it, and wants nothing more than to head back to New York. Then there's the new coach, a stubborn, opinionated, irritating man with superiority issues and questionable music taste. Butting heads with Rowen becomes the new normal, but it comes with passionate debate and an all-consuming lust.

Challenged to rebuild one of the worst teams in the league into a future cup contender, Rowen can't pass up the opportunity. Never in his twenty years of hockey has he ever seen a team managed so badly or coached players overflowing with resentment and bigotry. Yet there's something about this team and this city that compels him to roll up his sleeves and start dismantling. If only Mark, one of three siblings who now own the Raptors, wasn't so damned rock-headed yet so damned appealing his job might be easier. It doesn't look like either is willing to give in, but one night in a dark, desert hotel changes everything.

Coast To Coast

Arizona Raptors (Hockey Romance)

LA Storm

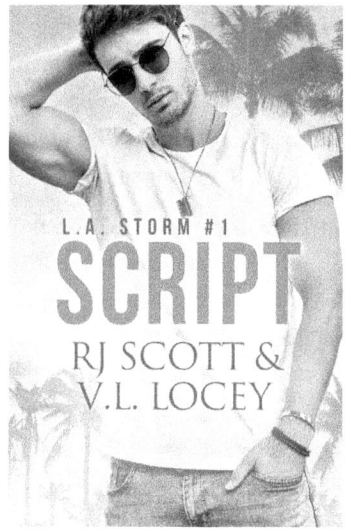

Script (LA Storm, 1)

Script

Hollywood A-lister Finn might be Canadian, but he needs Cameron to show him how to hockey.

Actor Finn Kerrigan is at a crossroads. After growing up a soap star, then starring in a hugely successful trilogy of action movies, he's finally given the chance to read a heartfelt and passionate script that could change his life forever. The role would be enough for people to see him as a serious actor, and maybe even win him an award or two (and no, a golden raspberry award for his action movies doesn't count). Once established as a serious actor he's sure he can come out of the closet and finally live his truth. When he lies to get the part of a hockey player on a struggling team, he suddenly has nowhere to hide. He might be Canadian, but the last time he skated he was ten, and no, he doesn't have hockey in his blood. With only a month until filming starts, he about to be exposed, but partnered with a player who's supposed to be giving him tips, he doesn't realize how many of his secrets will come to light. Falling in lust, one heated kiss at a time, is inevitable, but giving Cameron up at the end of the shoot could break his heart.

Cameron Chavkin is the face of the LA Storm. And the body, and the hair, and the smile. He's at the prime of his career, men and women want to be with him, and he's skating better than he ever has before. His house sits next to a famous rock star's mansion, his garage is filled with expensive cars, and he's even been asked to mentor a once-famous actor in a new hockey movie. Life is pretty sweet. Until the bad boy of hockey meets Finn, a man on the edge with more secrets than Cameron has endorsements. Knowing better than to get involved, Cameron is swept up despite himself, and when it's time to say goodbye to the Storm's most eligible bachelor is finding it hard to follow the script.

Script

LA Storm

Off The Ice (Chesterford Coyotes, 1)

Off The Ice

A coming-of-age love story with high school, hockey rivalry, friendship, family, and coming out.

Soren's life changes in an instant when he and his younger brother are adopted by hockey royalty. Making sense of his new life is hard enough, but when he's enrolled in a private school it means facing a whole new set of problems. Navigating friendship, family, and hockey is one thing, but being attracted to the boy who vexes him is a whole new thing.

Felix has a reputation to protect. He's the kid who seems to have everything but looks can be deceiving. Spinning lies about his perfect life, he's created a fantasy world that even he has started to believe. Only, it's not long before everything crumbles, all of his pretty lies are revealed, and only his closest rival sees through his pain and stands by him.

Fighting is easy, friendship is hard, but love is everything.

Off The Ice

Chesterford Coyotes

Also By RJ Scott

For a full list of ebooks and links please scan the code above or visit rjscott.co.uk/rjbooks

Meet RJ Scott

RJ discovered romance in books at a very young age and realized that if there wasn't romance on the page, she could create it in her head. With over one hundred and fifty books published, she is a full time author of gay romance.

She lives and works out of her home in the beautiful English countryside, spends her spare time reading, watching films, and enjoying time with her family.

The last time she had a week's break from writing she didn't like it one little bit and has yet to meet a box of chocolates she couldn't defeat.

www.rjscott.co.uk | rj@rjscott.co.uk

NEWSLETTER - rjscott.co.uk/rjnews

facebook.com/author.rjscott

x.com/Rjscott_author

instagram.com/rjscott_author

amazon.com/author/rj-scott

bookbub.com/authors/rj-scott

goodreads.com/rjscott

pinterest.com/rjscottauthor

Also By VL Locey

For a full list of ebooks and links please scan the code above or visit vllocey.com/stories-from-vl-locey

Meet V.L. Locey

V.L. Locey loves worn jeans, yoga, belly laughs, walking, reading and writing lusty tales, Greek mythology, the New York Rangers, comic books, and coffee.

(Not necessarily in that order.)

She shares her life with her husband, her daughter, one dog, two cats, a flock of assorted domestic fowl, and two Jersey steers.

When not writing spicy romances, she enjoys spending her day with her menagerie in the rolling hills of Pennsylvania with a cup of fresh java in hand.

vllocey.com
vicki@vllocey.com

Newsletter - vllocey.com/newsletter

facebook.com/V.L.Locey

x.com/vllocey

instagram.com/vl_locey

bookbub.com/authors/v-l-locey

goodreads.com/vllocey

pinterest.com/vllocey